"Jenny ... he shu...

Her anger ... had happened between them. ... want to hear some made-up story. What do you do, lust after anything in a skirt? Me one night, Naomi the next?"

"Naomi is business." His voice was hard.

"And what am I? Perks? That's what you said. How do you keep it all straight?"

"I have no trouble keeping it straight."

He drew her to him. Jenny held herself stiffly but was soon lost in the touch of him, his mouth against hers, his fingers tangled in her hair. It was intoxicating— her head was spinning. Time stood still.

When he finally released her, she pulled back, glaring—angry with him and with herself for responding. "Anyone handy will do, right?" she snapped.

Barbara McMahon and her two daughters share their home in the San Francisco Bay area with one dog, two cats and a pair of rabbits. Before settling down to work for a computer software company, her stint as an airline stewardess took her all over the world. But her favorite place remains the Sierra Nevada mountains where one day she hopes to live and write full-time.

Books by Barbara McMahon

Winter Stranger, Summer Lover

Barbara McMahon

Harlequin Books

TORONTO • NEW YORK • LONDON
AMSTERDAM • PARIS • SYDNEY • HAMBURG
STOCKHOLM • ATHENS • TOKYO • MILAN

ISBN 0-373-02895-4

Harlequin Romance first edition March 1988

Printed in U.S.A.

CHAPTER ONE

JENNY closed the book, a soft smile on her face. She liked happy endings. She was glad the book had ended on a high note; that the heroine had attained her goal, saved her father and still had been able to marry her sweetheart. She sighed, wishing real life was so ordered, that everyone lived happily ever after.

Slipping her legs from under the afghan, she stood up in the cold room. A nightly routine of hot chocolate before going to sleep was hard to shake. It was cold out of bed, but once she had had her chocolate, she could snuggle down in the warm covers and go to sleep.

Quickly she thrust her feet in her slippers and drew her warm woollen robe closer. She would make a quick trip to the kitchen.

It was cooler still in the hall as she left her warm bedroom. Winter was at its peak and she tried to economise by not heating the entire house, only the rooms she really needed. Summer was a different matter; the high elevation kept the house cool, and all the windows could be opened to enjoy the scented air of the Sierra Nevada. She didn't have a high electricity bill in summer, but the cold winter months were a different matter. Briefly she longed for the days when it had been easier to keep the house warm.

Descending the stairs, she shivered a little. It felt even colder than usual through her robe, her slippers not keeping the chill from her feet. Maybe she should turn the heat up a little, despite the cost. It had been snowing heavily since the late afternoon, and the temperature continued to drop. She went to the front door and flicked on the outside light. Opening the heavy wooden door a little, peeping through the crack, Jenny was surprised at how much snow there was on the ground, already more than a foot had fallen since it had started. If it continued, she would be snowbound for a few days. Her road was not one of the primary ones. It was often one of the last cleared by the snow ploughs.

Well, she thought, turning off the light and relatching the door, it wouldn't be the first time she had been snowbound. She had plenty of provisions and fuel, she'd be fine.

Softly she padded down the hall, turning on the light, opening the door to the kitchen. She flicked on that light and paused. Reflecting later, she realised she had not been afraid at that first moment, more startled than anything else.

The man was dressed all in black: black cords, a black jacket, similar to the kind sailors used to wear, Jenny thought as she took in his appearance. His hair was black, his eyes dark. He was sitting on the floor, leaning against her back door, dripping water on the linoleum. She registered the broken pane in the top part of the door, obviously his means of entry into her locked house.

She swallowed, not moving, shock rendering her immobile.

'Move easy, ma'am,' he said softly. 'Whatever you came here for, just do it. There may be people watching from outside and I don't want them to get suspicious.'

She nodded, the heavy thumping in her chest painful. She could scarcely breath as she tore her eyes away from him, moving stiffly to the stove to get the kettle. Filling it with water, she put it on the ring and turned on the gas. Who was he? What did he want? Shivering a little from the cold, a little from fear, Jenny hugged her arms across her chest, licked her lips. Was it all a bad dream?

'Who are you, and why are you here?' she asked, pleased her voice didn't quaver as she had thought it would. Trying not to look over to him, she moved slowly to get the cup and cocoa.

'I'm here because I was about to freeze to death in this blasted blizzard. There are a few of your neighbours looking for me and I don't intend for them to find me. Your house loomed up out of the snow, and I made use of it.'

'You're letting all my heat out of that broken pane. Not to mention the mess you're making on my kitchen floor. Why are you so wet?' Jenny shook her head. Why ask such mundane questions? Why are you here? she wanted to shout. What do you want of me?

His soft chuckle surprised her, but she kept her eyes resolutely on the cocoa she was spooning into her cup.

'I've been in the blizzard since shortly after noon, and lost my way. All the landmarks I had are gone, everything is covered in white. I was like a snowman when I came in, and it's all melting now. The house was dark. I thought it was empty. You alone in the house?'

Jenny felt a small shock of hope. Could she bluff him, make him think there was someone upstairs? Make him leave before discovering there was not? What would he do if he found she was alone? It wouldn't take long to realise she was. Bravely, defiantly, she turned to face him.

'I'm alone and I don't want you here. Would you please leave the way you came? You're warm now and can...' she trailed off as he slowly shook his head.

'I'm not going anywhere tonight, nor is anyone else. Have you seen how deep it is out there? I'd die of exposure before morning. Oh, no, lady, I'm not leaving.'

She stared at him silently, her mind whirling with questions, her stomach churning with apprehension. Who was he? Why was he here? Jenny lived miles from the nearest town. And it was a small community, she knew everyone. What neighbour was after him? No one, Jenny suspected. It was too late, anyone she knew would be home on a night like tonight.

The whistle on the kettle gave its piercing shrill, and Jenny turned to finish preparing her cocoa, a plan formulating in her mind. If she could leave him in the kitchen, she could get to the phone and call the Sheriff. Let someone know she was in trouble, alert someone to come for this intruder. She took a deep breath, the plan steadying her a little. Now her fear was that he'd read her mind. She glanced at him. He was still sitting on the floor, legs stretched out before him, leaning against the door, watching her closely.

'Where's your husband?' he asked.

Jenny blinked and stirred her hot drink. Another idea, pretend Johnny was coming later. Would that get rid of him?

'He's out. But I expect him home soon.'

'Not in this weather.'

'We have a four-wheel-drive vehicle, it can get through. I've done all I need to do in the kitchen. Do you still think someone is watching me?'

'I don't know. Just leave as you would if you were alone.'

'Goodnight,' she said, out of habit. She shook her head—why be polite to an intruder, a house-breaker?

Jenny carried her cup carefully. She had not filled it to the top, so she would be able to move rapidly once she was out of the kitchen, but there was no use letting this man know that. As if it were full to the brim, she walked slowly, carefully. Reaching the door, she flicked out the light and closed it, breaking into a run to reach the phone.

Snatching up the receiver, she pressed the "0" just as a warm hand covered hers on the receiver. She felt the shock like a kick in the stomach. He depressed the cradle, severing the connection. He had moved quickly, and silently. Backing away, her eyes wide, Jenny took a deep breath, tried to calm her racing heart, tears of frustration filled her eyes.

'No,' he said gently. Removing the phone from her grasp, he released the button, listening for a moment. 'It's dead, anyway.' He hesitated a moment, indecision touching his face briefly, then yanked the wire from the wall.

'Can't take a chance they'll fix it before morning. Do you have any more?'

Jenny licked her lips. 'One in my bedroom,' she said, at long last.

'Upstairs?'

She slowly nodded, her face clouding with worry. If the phone lines were down, there was no hope. He'd find the other phone, destroy it, too. Even if the phones came back on, she wouldn't be able to call for help. She thought briefly of making a dash to her room, but there would be no sanctuary there. There wasn't even a lock on the door. She had never needed one before.

'Let's go,' he said, pointing to the stairs.

Jenny turned and slowly started moving, holding her cup carefully. She felt as if she were in a nightmare. Would she awaken and find that it was just a dream? No, it was real enough: the cold was chilling, the slow, fearful thud of her heart in her chest a painful reminder of the intruder and the fear he caused.

Jenny had her foot on the first step when they heard the rumble of a truck, voices outside. She paused, hope flaring again and looked over her shoulder, up to the face of the man. He was tall, over six feet, and seemed to be looming over her own five foot five inches.

'Wait,' he said, moving to the heavy front door, ear cocked to better hear the voices. In only a couple of moments, there was a rap at her door.

Jenny moved to stand by the door, her heart skipping. Was this help? She threw a glance at the stranger.

'One wrong move and one of your friends might get hurt,' he said softly, moving back a few feet, eyes narrowed as he watched her.

The rap came again. Jenny reached out a shaky hand to flick on the outside light, release the locks and open the door a few inches.

'Yes? Oh, hi, Nate. What are you doing out on a night like this?'

'Hi, Jenny, it's awful, isn't it? Can I come in?'

She looked over to where the stranger was, but he had disappeared. Without making any noise, he had gone into the closed-off den, that door now open a crack. No doubt he could see and hear everything.

'Of course, come on in. What are you doing out so late? It's freezing out, still snowing, too, I see.'

Jenny tried to act normally, her eyes flickering involuntarily to the study door.

'Yes. Forecast is for lots more. Looks like we'll be snowed in for a while. You OK?' Nate Wilson was dressed in warm mountain gear, his hat and jacket caked with snow.

'Sure, did you come just to check on me?' She smiled at her neighbour. They had never been friends, but Nate had been a friend of Johnny's.

'No, me and Jim are looking for someone. A man, stranger to these parts. You seen anyone walking around, probably earlier?'

'Nate, it gets dark around five. Even earlier on a stormy day like today. If I saw someone this afternoon, he'd be long gone by now. It's after ten. Who is it, anyone I know?' Jenny was puzzled—why would Nate be looking for the stranger so late at night, and in such inclement weather?

'Yeah, I guess you're right, it's late. We were following his tracks, but the snow covered them. Lost him a few hours ago and we're just searching all around now.'

'What for? And why you and Jim? Why not Bob Marshall?' Bob Marshall was Alpine County's Sheriff.

'Well, it's not a—er—legal matter, really. Just a guy that—er—owes us some money from a poker game. Tried to welch on the deal. Won't keep you, Jenny. If you see anyone you don't know, give me or Jim a call.'

Jenny started to say something, tell him her line was down. Give some indication that all was not right. But the menace the intruder offered was too much. She nodded as she watched him leave. Her heart sank as she felt as if her last hope was leaving when Nate turned to go, but she was afraid to try and stop him. She would not jeopardise his safety, or her own. Not while the stranger stood nearby, watching their every move. She didn't know what he would be capable of, but he was big, strong-looking and threatening. If she went along with him, maybe he'd leave and things would be all right again.

Reluctantly, she shut the door, hearing Nate call to Jim, hearing them move off, out of earshot. Their truck revved in the hushed night, moving away. Slowly she turned to face the den. The door opened and the stranger stepped out.

'What's going on?' she asked. 'Nate and Jim don't wander all over creation in a near-blizzard, and hours after dark, to follow a guy who welched on some poker match.'

His lips twitched at her comment.

'No, there is more to it. You're a bright lady. Not your concern, though. They friends of yours?'

'I've known them both for years. We're all from Palmer.'

He nodded at the mention of the town that served as the local community for the residents of this portion of Alpine County. It was a small town, only a handful of residents lived in the town proper. Its store and post office serviced a large area of ranches, lumber camps, and quiet residences of the local populace.

'We were on our way upstairs, I believe.' He motioned her forwards.

The tight knot of fear filled her throat, almost choking her. Glancing around desperately, she sought some means of escape, some place to hide. There was none.

Jenny started up the steps, still balancing her now cold cocoa. As she moved, she could feel him follow her, close on her heels. She took a shaky breath and paused at the top, turned to face him.

'Please don't rip the phone from this wall. It's a modular one and can unplug,' she said, pausing as she frantically tried to find some way to delay him, to get away.

He shrugged. 'Whatever. I'll unplug it and throw it in the snow.'

Her fear gave way to anger as she flared up. 'Then just who is going to pay for it, and for the one downstairs? You can't just break into someone's home and wreck it, and expect to get away with it, you know. You have to assume some responsibility for your actions!'

He smiled again, and Jenny looked away, trying to hold on to her anger. His smile had the strangest effect on her. His teeth white against his brown skin, his eyes deep and intriguing. She would not let herself be beguiled by the good looks of the man, the charisma and magnetism of him. One minute she feared for her safety, the next minute for her sanity!

'Where's the phone?'

Jenny led the way to her room, pausing at the door as he moved past her and went straight to the telephone. Listening to it for a moment, he then unplugged it from the wall, and unplugged the wire from the receiver. Coiling the wire, he stuffed it into a pocket of his jacket.

'No problem, still dead, but no chances,' he said, turning to look at her, then surveyed the room, assessing it. 'When I leave, I'll give you back the cord.'

Jenny caught his measured look, and rushed into speech. 'Now you're safe for tonight. Can you leave my room, so I can go to bed?'

He looked back, arching one eyebrow.

'Alone?'

She frowned fiercely at him, 'Yes, alone!' Just what was he implying? What other thoughts did he have? She swallowed again as a small tickle of fear traced down her back. God, he wasn't suggesting ... She stepped back.

'My, my, I thought your husband was returning any moment.'

She was flustered, she'd forgotten. 'I mean alone now, of course. He'll be along. As you saw, Nate and Jim made it through, and so will Johnny.'

Could she get away with it? Would he leave if he thought her husband was coming? It was one thing to terrorise a young woman on her own, something else again to have to deal with another man. Not, she decided, looking at him, that he'd have much trouble with whomever it was.

He moved back to the door. 'I'm cold. Do you have a drier? My clothes are still wet and it will take for ever for them to dry in this cold weather.'

She smiled sweetly. 'Good, maybe you'll get pneumonia and leave me alone.'

'If I get pneumonia, you'll have to nurse me.'

'I wouldn't!'

He leaned closer, looking deep into Jenny's blue eyes, his a velvety brown, warm and soft. Jenny thought she would lose herself in the warmness of his gaze. She swallowed hard, resisting the urge to step back again.

'My guess is that you would,' he said softly. His dark eyes lit with amusement as he towered over her, his broad shoulders and height dwarfing Jenny, his eyes doing strange things to her emotions.

She stepped back, not wanting to be so close to him, turning to break the spell.

'There's a drier downstairs, off the kitchen. It's in a laundry room.' Just get out, go away!

'How large is your husband?'

The question took her off guard. 'Huh?'

'How large? Can I wear something of his while these things dry?'

Jenny knew a moment of panic. 'I—er—he's small. Not much bigger than I am.' She was trying to think of something to give him, get him away. Get him off this line of questioning before he realised the truth.

'I . . . there's a bathrobe you could use. But you should hurry, he'll be along soon.' She moved slowly to the closet, opened the door a little and reached in for a large blue terry-cloth bathrobe. It was large on her, but would be much too small to fit the stranger. Still, it would be adequate until his own clothes were dry. She thrust it at him.

He took it, glancing around again.

'Mind if I take a shower, too?' he drawled.

She was momentarily off guard. Maybe he didn't mean to harm her after all, just get dry and warm. Maybe things would be OK and he'd leave when he was through.

'I don't care what you do as long as you get out of this room,' she said, glaring at him.

'Will I have time before your husband gets home?' he said, watching her closely.

'I hope not!' She turned away, willing him to leave, wishing she could push him out the door, out of her home.

'I might chance it.' He left the room, closing the door quietly behind him.

Jenny moved to sit on the edge of the bed, straining to hear him, hear where he was, trying to envision what he was doing. She looked around her bedroom. There was nothing with which to wedge the door shut, nothing she could place as a barrier to his returning if he so chose. How she wished she had a lock for the door.

The noise from the bathroom penetrated her thoughts. He *was* taking a shower. Of all the nerve, first to break in, now this!

Could she sneak in and surprise him, overpower him while he was not expecting her? She rose, then realised he probably would have locked that door—that room did have a lock. Anyway, once she had done it, what was she to do; find something to tie him up with, try to stay awake until someone else arrived, watching him all the time until she could be rid of him? Turning him out would not work; he had no qualms about breaking her windows, he'd just come back in from another opening. And would probably be angry, too.

She pondered various plans, discarding one after another, trying for something, anything, nothing coming to mind that she felt would work under the circumstances. Maybe she would be OK; he'd left her alone so far.

'My clothes should be dry soon.' His voice came from the door.

Jenny looked up in fright, her throat going dry, her eyes wide. Framed in the opening was the intruder, long legs below the short terry robe, broad shoulders straining the material, the robe barely covering him, open at the throat.

He stepped in. 'Where's your husband?' he asked, moving close to the bed, looking down at her.

'He'll be along soon, had to go to—um—to Lake Tahoe on business.'

'No, there's no man living here. There are no clothes in the cupboard, no razor or aftershave in the bathroom. No signs of a man.'

Jenny's eyes dropped. Her bluff hadn't worked.

'You're right,' she said slowly. 'He was killed in a car accident about a year ago. He won't ... he's never coming home again.'

The first fierce hurt and anguish had diminished. It had been over a year now since she had been told the news, been stunned by it. The last year had been hard, but Jenny was over the worst, now. Settled with life, going on.

'So now you know. There will be no one else coming.' She twisted her wedding ring nervously, round and round. What now? Now that he knew she was alone?

'I'll be gone in the morning,' he said softly. 'You'll be safe. I'm not going to hurt you.'

For some reason, his words comforted her. She felt relieved, reassured. Maybe, just maybe she *would* be all right, if she could believe him. She looked up at the stranger, and a small smile tugged at her mouth.

'You don't look like a villain in that get-up,' she said. The scanty terry-cloth robe scarcely covering his body, his long, powerful legs beneath the short cover gave him a comical look. She felt less afraid.

He smiled back. 'Didn't you know? I'm not the villain, I'm the hero!'

CHAPTER TWO

JENNY watched as he turned and left the room, drawing the door shut behind him. Hero, indeed, she thought scornfully. Just who did he think he was? She drew a deep breath, trying to calm down. Was he coming back? The minutes dragged by.

Yawning, she crossed carefully, silently, to her window, drawing the curtains to one side, peering out. It looked as if it were still snowing, from the little she could see reflected in the light from her window. She turned back, anxious to get into bed and get to sleep, seek oblivion from the nightmare in which she found herself.

She grimaced at her now cold chocolate; how she longed for her cup of warm cocoa, but she would not venture out again! The old adage was true—ignorance was bliss. Had she not left her warm bed a little while ago, she'd still be blissfully unaware of the stranger's presence. Would he have stayed downstairs all night? Could she have avoided any knowledge of him except a broken window found in the morning?

If it would stop snowing soon, maybe the stranger would leave in the morning. Go on to wherever he was heading and leave her in peace. She sighed, unfastening her robe. She'd be better able to cope in the morning.

The click of her door jerked her head around. The stranger, fully clothed once more, stood in the frame, his arms full of blankets and a pillow. Jenny recognised the yellow blanket and coverlet from the bed in her guest room.

'What are you doing?' she asked, drawing the robe close again.

'Just got some covers for the night. It's cool in here.'

'What do you mean, *in here*?' A touch of fear coursed through her.

He paused, dumped the blankets on the floor and shut the door. 'I'm tired. I want to go to sleep,' he explained patiently, as if to a child. 'It's not warm enough to sleep without some covers, so I got these.'

'Well, take them back where you found them. Sleep in there!'

He shook his head. 'Can't do that. Want to make sure you don't try something in the night. I wouldn't hear you from the other room.'

Jenny's surprise showed. 'Try something? Like what?' Had he read her mind earlier?

'Don't know, signal a neighbour, try to get out and go into town.'

'On a night like this? You're nuts!'

Shrugging his broad shoulders, he bent to smooth one blanket out, placing the pillow at one end. 'Nevertheless, I'll just sleep in here tonight.'

Jenny watched in disbelief as he stretched out on the floor and covered himself with the yellow blanket and coverlet.

'I'm a light sleeper, by the way,' he said as he drew the cover over his jeans, across his chest and up against the pillow. 'Goodnight, Jenny,' he said softly.

Jenny glanced frantically about, as if seeking something that would enable her to get rid of her unwanted room-mate, but saw nothing remotely helpful. She glared at him, to no avail. He had his eyes closed already, his breathing was even.

With an angry flounce, she turned off the lights, holding her breath to see if he moved. After a long moment of straining her ears, she relaxed, slowly eased off her bathrobe and climbed into bed. She lay back, straining to detect any movement, any sound indicating that he was moving. He had not touched her except for taking the phone. He had said he wouldn't harm her, but could she believe him?

She held her breath again, listening to his slow, even breath. If the rhythm was any indication, he was already asleep. Closing her eyes, Jenny was again reminded poignantly of her husband. On one or two nights after they had been married and she had not been able to sleep, she had found such comfort in lying in the dark listening to Johnny's steady breathing. How like, yet how different the sound of the stranger. It was nice, sharing with someone else.

Jenny's eyes flew open. What was she thinking of? She wanted him out of her house, out of her life! He'd leave in the morning. She'd see to it, somehow. Daylight would offer a way.

On that hopeful note, she fell asleep.

When morning came, Jenny almost thought she had dreamed the whole escapade. She rose at her usual time and glanced out of the window. The sky was still overcast. The snow had stopped, but lay heavy on the trees, the road, the pavement. As she dressed, she went over the events of last night. Of the stranger there was no sign. Maybe he had left already. Maybe she would not need to see him again. Curiously, she felt a small pang of disappointment at this thought.

Jenny dressed quickly, pulling on blue jeans, a soft blue sweater and warm boots. She brushed her hair until it shone, the light brown colour highlighted by warm, blonde streaks, even in winter. Set for the day, she ran lightly down the steps. Pushing her way into the kitchen, her eyes flew to the spot before the door where she had first seen him. It was empty. The broken pane was patched with paper, the room warm, as a kettle boiled merrily on the stove.

Jenny looked around. The stranger was sitting at the breakfast table, tipped back in his chair, lazily watching her.

'Hi,' he said easily.

'Hi,' she replied stiffly. He wasn't as fearful in the light of day, and Jenny felt better able to cope. Moving into the room, she went to the table, sat gingerly on one of the chairs. 'Do you have a name?'

He smiled. 'Sure. Kyle Martin. What's yours?'

'You called me by it last night.'

'Jenny. Jenny what?'

'Warwick.' She glanced out the window. The snow was deeper than she had thought. 'You leaving this morning?'

He shook his head. 'I doubt it. How can I get anywhere in that mess?'

'Walk.'

He shook his head again. 'No, I'd freeze before I got a mile away. It's cold out and the snow is almost three feet deep in spots.'

'Well, you can't stay here!'

'I think I can. I did last night. Anyway, I don't want to get into an argument with you. I plan to stay, so make up your mind to it.'

Jenny glared at him.

The shrill whistle of the kettle broke into her thoughts. Out of habit she rose and took it from the fire.

'I'd fix coffee, but I don't know where you keep it,' Kyle drawled, watching her.

'Am I expected to wait on you, too, while you're here?'

'Come now, Jenny, you have to eat, how much trouble to fix a little extra for me?' he said reasonably.

'Look, Mr Kyle Martin, just who are you and why are you breaking into people's houses, hiding? I don't want you here. Can't you find somewhere else to go?'

'I'm visiting this area incognito, you might say. I don't want certain people to know.'

'Oh, that's clear. Who? Nate and Jim? Was there a poker game?'

'No, there was no poker game.'

The silence after that statement dragged on and on. Jenny, waiting for further explanation, Kyle silent, watching her. Finally her impatience bubbled over.

'Well, why don't you want Nate to know you're here?'

'It's long and involved and doesn't concern you. At least, I hope it doesn't. It's not that I don't want your friend Nate to know. I don't want anyone to know.' He rose, towering over her. 'I'd forget asking questions about things that don't concern you. Are you going to fix us breakfast?'

Her emotions seething, Jenny turned and began to get things out for the meal. What was going on? How was this guy connected to Nate and Jim? Why had they been out looking for Kyle late last night? And why didn't he want anyone to know he was here?

She drew the cups she needed for the coffee from the cupboard. Slamming one down before Kyle, spilling a little, she kept her eyes away from him. He sank slowly back into his chair, drawing the cup near him. Jenny quickly gathered the things she wanted for breakfast—eggs, bacon, bread, milk. All the while she prepared the meal, she was conscious of his steady gaze on her, her thoughts spinning. What was going on? Finally, frustration rising, she turned to him.

'Do you have to watch my every move?'

Kyle shrugged, a smile lurking in his eyes. 'More interesting than watching the wall.'

'Well, I don't like it. Look somewhere else!'

'I'll look where I want. Unless you want to try to make me look elsewhere?'

'You're making me nervous,' she muttered, turning back to the eggs. His eyes were unnerving, his very presence unnerving.

In spite of his constant regard, she finished preparing the meal. Disdainfully placing his plate before him, she sat opposite. Eating with her eyes firmly on her plate, she tried to regain her composure. Surely he'd go soon, he had to!

Kyle kept half an eye on Jenny as he ate. The meal was eaten in silence, only when he was finished did he speak.

'That was delicious. Is there more coffee?'

Jenny rose and took his cup, filling it and handing him the full cup. She tried to glare at him, only to be confused by the amused regard she met when her eyes locked with his.

'Did you say you have a four-wheel-drive vehicle?' he asked.

Warily Jenny looked back. 'Yes. Why, are you planning to steal it?'

'Can it get me out of here?' He ignored her comment.

She sighed and rose to go to the window. Looking out, she surveyed her yard. The snow had stopped during the night, after blanketing the landscape. It was over a foot deep, higher in some areas where it had been blown into drifts. The trees were heavy with snow, branches bowed beneath the weight. She tried to see where her driveway was. Surely CalTrans had cleared the highway by now, and if her truck made it to the road, he could get away. She turned back.

'I think it could make it to the highway.' She licked her lips, waiting for his response.

'Can you drive me out?'

Jenny was surprised. 'Me? I thought you would take the truck.'

'I'm not into grand theft, and if I took it I don't know how to get it back to you. Besides, I don't have much experience driving in snow. If you've lived here, chances are you do have the experience necessary to get us out.'

'You want me to take you to the highway?' Was that where his car was? Or had he parked it in town? Could he have walked all that way yesterday in the storm? And why had he been out in the storm in the first place? Who *was* he?

'No, not the highway, to Strawberry.'

'Strawberry? Palmer is closer.'

'Exactly. I want to go to Strawberry.'

'And you'll be gone?'

'Never saw such a hospitable lady! Are you always so anxious for guests to leave?'

'Not invited ones. You're hardly a guest.'

'I could stay.'

'No, I can take you to Strawberry. Ready now?'

Kyle chuckled at her quick response. Jenny felt her heart lurch at his lop-sided smile, the way his eyes crinkled. The tan he had was evidence of much time spent out of doors, even in winter. He was certainly an attractive man, in a slightly rakish way. What was he up to? In other circumstances she might have been interested in learning more about him. Now she was only interested in getting him away from her home.

She watched him as he rose. How tall he was, built like an athlete. There was no superfluous flesh on the man: his shoulders were broad, his chest large, his legs long. He was trim, graceful, dynamic.

'Know me again?' he mocked.

She blushed and turned away, vexed that he had caught her looking at him. Hearing his chuckle only made her blush more. She busied herself clearing the table.

Kyle left the room and she was alone. Quickly she ran water over the dishes. She'd wait to wash them when she got back. Strawberry wasn't far. It wouldn't take her long to get rid of him. At least he wasn't stealing her truck.

When she went to the hall cupboard to get her parka, Kyle was running lightly down the stairs, his thick wool jacket over his arm. Jenny looked quickly away.

The truck started right up, for which she was thankful. Jenny put it in four-wheel drive and slowly backed out. Once out of the garage, she put it in low and eased forward.

Watching carefully for landmarks, she tried to keep to the driveway, though it was almost impossible to tell where it was. Clenching the steering wheel tightly, she kept the truck at a steady ten miles an hour. Occasionally they would skid, but Jenny would coax the big pick-up back on to what she thought was the lane. Steadily she kept on, hardly aware of the silent man at her side, intent only on keeping the truck moving, trying to determine where she was, where the lane was. Her house was over a mile from the highway, but the drive seemed much longer. Slowly they moved, the truck crunching down the snow, pushing it aside, moving forward, lurching, sliding, moving constantly.

The highway came into view. It had been ploughed, the snowblower distributing the snow on either side of the highway, but not clearing the roadside entirely. The snow was deeper here, twice the truck stuck, lurched, moved again. Jenny was perspiring beneath her parka, her eyes aching with the strain, her hands clenched on the wheel. Only a little further, she repeated, then we'll be OK.

Finally they tilted down, reached the ploughed road. In comparison to the deep snow they had been going over, the road seemed clear and easy. Gradually she picked up speed until she was going over twenty-five. Settling down at that safe speed, she relaxed a little, eased the tense muscles at her shoulders.

'You're good,' Kyle murmured gently at her side. He was attentive now, watching before them and behind, as if searching for his pursuers.

Jenny gave a reluctant look in the rear-view mirror. She wished she were heading for Palmer, instead of Strawberry. A quick trip to the Sheriff's office and her unwanted intruder would be guest of the county. She frowned—where was the police office in Strawberry? She tried to remember, but had never had a need for it before, and just didn't know where it was. Maybe she could find it. Risking a glance at Kyle, she tried to school her features so he wouldn't suspect what was whirling in her brain.

The trip to Strawberry was uneventful. Kyle didn't speak, but kept up his surveillance, glancing to Jenny once or twice as if to speak, then turning back to the window.

'Slow down here.' His voice startled her after the long silence. They were approaching the town. On the right side was a petrol station, just beyond, the other buildings of Strawberry began.

'I want you to drop me at the petrol station. Near the phone,' he said.

Jenny glanced at him, shrugged and slowed to turn into the station. It had been cleared and she easily brought the truck near the phone. Stopping she looked at him.

'Jenny——' He stopped, glanced around. There was not a sign of another person.

'Goodbye, Kyle Martin. You'll understand if I don't say, drop in any time.'

He smiled at that.

'You know,' he said, turning to face her, 'I appreciate your reluctant hospitality. Also——' He reached out his hands and cupped her face, his thumbs caressing her rosy cheeks.

Jenny caught her breath at his touch, mesmerised by his eyes, soft velvet brown gazing warmly down into hers. He bent his head and put his lips against hers in a warm kiss.

His lips were cool, warming as they rested against hers, moving a little as he took his time with the kiss. Jenny's heart raced at his touch, her hands grasping the wheel to keep from putting them around this intruder. Slowly Kyle raised his head, smiling down at Jenny.

'I've wanted to do that since I first saw you last night. Goodbye, sweet Jenny.'

She didn't reply, just watched as he got out of the truck, glanced quickly around and went to the phone. Slowly she put the truck in gear and drove off. Glancing once in her mirror, she began her search for the police station. On the third cross street was the small sign, pointing to it. She looked back as she began her turn. There was no sign of the tall man dressed in black.

Jenny pulled up before the police station and stopped. Turning off the engine, she sat and stared into space. What good would it do to go in? Would they believe her? If he wasn't in the phone-box, would they be able to find him? He hadn't really hurt her, only frightened her a little. There was no lasting harm done. Jenny frowned, she really didn't want him caught.

Her mind relived the kiss, a small smile tugging at her lips. It had been a long time since she had been kissed. Not that his kiss had meant anything. Anyway, he was gone. She shook her head and sighed. Reaching for the key, she started up and headed for home.

The dishes in the sink were waiting when she entered the kitchen. Without much thought, she slowly washed them up and dried them. Turning, she glanced to the table where Kyle had sat that morning. Gone now. Gone for good.

She shook off her reverie and headed for the den. It was cold, but she switched on the small space heater and soon was warm enough to work.

Jenny worked as a book-keeper for several small businesses in Palmer. Most of her work she did from her own home, going into town two or three times a week to the various offices she worked for, to collect the next assignments and leave what she'd completed. It was lonely sometimes, yet gave her a freedom she would not have had were she tied to an office from nine to five every day.

It was late when Jenny finished and went to bed. She locked the house carefully, though wondered why she bothered when there was only cardboard on the small pane near the back-door knob. She'd have to get that fixed as soon as someone could get out to her place. And, unless the snow melted soon, it would be a long time before someone from town could make it through.

Flicking on the light in her room, she wandered in, closing the door. Her eye was caught by the small pile on her pillow. Jenny went over. There was her phone wire, neatly coiled. Beside it was a folded note surrounding a folded currency bill.

Jenny reached out and picked it up.

'For the downstairs phone, and the broken window. Kyle.' The note was short, the handwriting bold and strong. Jenny unfolded the money—it was a fifty-dollar bill.

She smiled, sinking to the edge of her bed. He had said he would give her back her phone wire. And now he had made reparation for the damage he'd caused. A curious house-breaker! She was suddenly glad she had not turned him in at the police station.

'Good luck, Kyle Martin,' she murmured, remembering once again his kiss.

CHAPTER THREE

As time went by, Jenny found herself thinking about the dark stranger who had invaded her home. She had long stopped dwelling on her dead husband, and wishing things were different than they were. Time healed all wounds, just as her mother had told her. She still missed Johnny, might always miss him, but instead of thinking endlessly about him her thoughts revolved around more recent events. Remembering the night Kyle Martin had broken into her home; the breakfast they had shared; their ride to Strawberry. Always ending with the kiss he'd given her. She wove fantasies in which they met under different circumstances, and . . .

That was where Jenny would get bogged down. She knew nothing about him.

There were so many questions she had about that night. Why had he been out in one of the worst storms of winter? Where had he been going, and why? Obviously a stubborn man—why else persevere through a blizzard? Making up one answer after another, Jenny discarded them. She could not think of a compelling enough reason.

Nate and Jim must know, however. They, too, had been out in the storm, yet Jenny could hardly ask them too much without revealing she'd known about the stranger, after all.

As time passed, it was more and more difficult to bring up the topic. Questions would have been asked of her as to why she hadn't reported the break-in, why hadn't she contacted the Sheriff? She didn't want to have to explain, wasn't sure she *could* explain. But time didn't diminish her thoughts of Kyle.

Would things be different today if she had talked with him more, questioned him further, found out more about him? Why couldn't she put him from her mind—was it the mystery that kept her thinking about him? No, just foolish daydreams. She would do better to forget him entirely, so she told herself over and over.

A month after the break-in, Jenny was working in her den. The snow was still piled high around her house, the drive ploughed, spring a month or more away. She was rocking back in her chair, gazing out at the white landscape, resting her eyes from the tedious calculations she had just completed. It was quiet, peaceful. Maybe she'd take a day off and go skiing tomorrow. She was current with all her clients. A day away from the house would be good.

The vision of a pair of warm brown eyes, smiling down at her, swam before her face. Did *he* ski? The tan he had had indicated time spent outside—maybe she'd see him at the ski resort. Frowning, she pushed the image away. Time enough now to stop day-dreaming about Kyle Martin. If he had been anything besides a charming house-breaker, if he had had any interest in furthering their acquaintance, she might have heard from him by now. After all, he knew where she lived. She picked up her pencil.

She heard the sound of the engine as it droned closer and closer. Company? She rose and went to her front door, opening it and going out on to the porch. It was cold, but sunny. Shivering a little in the crisp air, she watched as a large pick-up truck drew up and stopped. A weathered old man climbed out and smiled at her.

'You Jenny Warwick?' he called.

She nodded.

'I've got something for you.'

'For me?' He didn't look like a delivery man, and she wasn't expecting anything.

He nodded and reached back inside the truck. A large German Shepherd dog jumped down, gazing up at the old man, waiting for his command. At a swift cupping motion of the man's hand, the dog fell into step beside him. The two of them walked to the porch. Another small motion, and the dog sat.

'I'm to say, "For you, to keep you company, and to protect you from other midnight intruders".' He smiled up at Jenny.

She caught her bottom lip between her teeth, a warm glow spreading through her as she looked down at the lovely dog. A bubble of laughter welled up. The arrogance of the man! Breaking into her home, now sending her a watch-dog. A warm feeling pervaded her. Kyle Martin had not forgotten her; he had sent her protection, though long after the fact. She looked at the man.

'Thank you. Won't you come in? Where's Kyle? What's he up to now?' Was he still breaking into lonely, isolated houses, she wondered. Why?

As they went inside, the dog right beside the man, he shook his head.

''Fraid I don't know any Kyle, ma'am. Might be the man who bought the dog, but he paid cash and I don't know his name. Came about a week ago, looked over all my dogs, picked out this one especially. Said he'd suit you.' He reached down to pat the dog. 'He's one of my best. Name's Shasta.'

'Hi, Shasta.' Jenny slowly held out her hand, letting the dog sniff her before gently patting him. She dropped to her knees and smiled at the dog. 'He's beautiful!'

'Trained, too. The man who bought him wanted that in a dog. I've got books in the car which will tell you how to keep him, how he's been trained. You won't have any trouble with Shasta.'

'Thank you, Mr——?'

'Ben Johnson.'

'Thank you, Mr Johnson.' Jenny stood up. 'Can I get you some coffee?'

'That would be right nice.'

While they had coffee, Jenny, hoping her voice was casual, asked him again about the man who had purchased the dog.

'Tall, he was. Tall and dark. Nothing much to notice about him. Was very specific about where you were, about my bringing the dog. Usually whoever buys one takes them home. This one I had to deliver.'

Jenny was conscious of a vague disappointment. She wished Kyle had brought Shasta himself. Why hadn't he? Didn't he want to see her again? Still, she smiled as she looked at her dog, the thought was what counted. She was torn between being exasperated at the nerve of the man, and the delight in her new present. Delight won.

Ben Johnson spent an hour with Jenny, showing her how to put the dog through his paces, how to have him heel, sit, stay, lie down. Voice commands and hand signals were gone over until Jenny had a good feel for them.

'Leaving you the books, too. You won't forget.'

'No, I'll use them all the time. Thank you, Mr Johnson.'

'My pleasure, ma'am. Must be going now.'

Jenny turned to Shasta when the truck was lost to sight.

'So, he sent you to guard me. If you only knew how funny that was. Well, we'll be great friends, my pretty dog.' As Shasta watched her talking, he slowly wagged his tail. Jenny smiled and turned to let them back into the house.

As spring came to the Sierra Nevada, Jenny spent long hours out of doors, walking with Shasta, exploring the woods, jogging along the roads, practising the commands, learning more and more about the large dog. She did feel protected by his presence. He slept in her room at night, stayed near her during the day. And she found Shasta good company, especially after the long year since Johnny's death.

She never heard further from Kyle Martin, though she ran into Nate Wilson in town one day and couldn't resist asking him about his search in the storm.

'Never did find him, guess he left town.' Nate was uncomfortable, and changed the topic of conversation. Jenny was puzzled: what was the connection between the two of them?

Another day she was stopped by George Carlisle. George owned one of the largest ranches in the area. While Jenny and George's younger brother had been in the same grade in school, Jenny knew George only slightly.

'So, Jenny Warwick! How are you?' George smiled genially, stopping to chat with her before climbing into his car.

'I'm doing fine, thanks. How's Nick?'

'Still likes forestry work. Oregon suits him. I see you're starting to get out more.'

'Winter is hardly the time to go around,' she smiled.

'Getting over Johnny?' he asked gently.

'Yes. I still miss him, but the worst is over.'

'I'm glad. Maybe we could have dinner one evening.'

'I'd like that.' She smiled and moved away as he climbed into his car. She considered the possibility of going out with George. She didn't know him well, and was a little surprised when he had showed an interest in her. Maybe he was just being neighbourly. She had been a bit of a recluse since Johnny was killed. It would do her good to get out again.

Spring came and with it long walks in the woods with Shasta. The dog quickly learned his territory and would roam the area around the home when let out, never going far, always returning promptly when Jenny called.

They enjoyed hiking further from home. Jenny was glad to get out in the fresh air, and glad for a companion on her walks. She was healthier and more fit than ever.

Her phone was ringing when Jenny got home one day from an excursion. She dashed in to grab it, slightly out of breath.

'Is this Jenny Warwick?' an unknown voice enquired.

'Yes. Who is this?'

'Stuart Brownley. We've never met, Mrs Warwick. I'll be in Palmer this afternoon and wondered if you could spare me a few minutes of your time. I work for the US Treasury Department.'

'Is this the IRS?'

He chuckled. 'No, Mrs Warwick. The Treasury Department has many branches. May I stop by and see you?'

Jenny was perplexed. She had no idea why someone from the Treasury Department would want to see her. If she wasn't going to be audited by the IRS, what could it be?

'What is this about, Mr Brownley?'

'I would rather explain in person, if it's all right with you.'

'I guess so. I'll be in all afternoon. Do you know where I live?'

'Yes. I should be there before three.'

Jenny hung up slowly, curious as to why the US Treasury Department wanted to talk to her. Why come to her? Wouldn't they ask her to come to their offices?

Shortly after two-thirty, a nondescript black sedan pulled into her driveway, drawing up close to the house. Jenny was watching from the front window, watched as the man walked up to her door. He was of average height, brown hair, brown suit. Brownley suited him.

She opened the door to his knock, Shasta at her left knee.

'Mrs Warwick?' He looked a little surprised.

'Yes. You're Mr Brownley?'

'Yes, I am. Sorry if I looked startled. I'm afraid I was expecting someone a little older; I understood that you were a widow. May I come in?'

Jenny nodded, opening the door wider.

As they sat down in the living-room, Brownley drew his wallet from his pocket, flipping it open. 'My identification.'

Jenny took it and read the card. He looked very like his picture. She handed it back.

'Your information is correct, I am a widow. What can I do for you, Mr Brownley?'

'I'll come straight to the point. My Department investigates drug abuse in the United States. My particular area is marijuana in California. I'm sure you've read about the large areas under cultivation.'

Jenny nodded. 'I thought it was in Mendocino County, though.'

'There is a lot there. Other areas, too. We've reason to suspect a good deal of it is being grown around here. Either on private land, or in the El Dorado National Forest. What we want to do is infiltrate the area and try to find where it is being grown, and by whom.'

'What do you expect from me? I don't know anyone growing marijuana. I don't even know what it looks like.'

'Well, I'm glad to hear that.' He smiled briefly. 'Actually, the Department would like to have one of our men here. What we need, however, is a cover. Small towns are notorious for excluding new-comers. Rather than take years to build a background, gain acceptance, we were hoping an established resident could provide the cover we need.'

'Why me?'

'Your house is rather isolated. Easier for our man to come and go as he pleases without nosy neighbours wondering what he's doing. You and your family have been residents of Palmer for years, respected, well liked. The perfect cover.'

She nodded. 'And the cover story?'

Brownley looked at her for a long moment. 'A visiting cousin?'

'No. I don't have any cousins. Everyone in town knows both my parents were only children. I'm an only child.' She thought a moment. 'Maybe a son of an old school-friend of my mom's. She has several friends from other areas of California. She's for ever going visiting.' Jenny shook her head. 'I don't know, though. A friend's son would stay with Mom, not me.'

'A cousin of your late husband?'

Jenny considered that, then slowly nodded. 'Yes, Johnny's dad had several brothers and sisters that live elsewhere. He's dead now, too, and Johnny's mother went to live with her sister in Sacramento.' She looked at him. 'Why would he come to stay with me, though?'

'He's a writer, needs a quiet place to work? Given to wandering around while thinking up the new plot-line?' Brownley suggested.

Jenny shrugged. 'If you think it will work. When will your agent be coming?'

'Actually, not for a few weeks. The reason I wanted to lay the groundwork is so you can start talking about your expected visitor. No use in springing this upon the town. That will cause as much talk as if our agent just pitched a tent in the town centre. We'd like you to begin telling people your husband's cousin is coming this summer, lay the foundation of his relationship to you, so to speak.'

'And how long will your agent stay?'

'Until we find out where the marijuana is and who might be responsible for its being here. It could be months, maybe only weeks. The Department will pick up the cost of housing him with you, of course.'

Jenny looked at her visitor, considering the implications of the proposal he had made. Then the thought of marijuana being grown near Palmer, the thought of all the havoc it could cause, helped her make up her mind.

'OK, Mr Brownley, I'll be glad to help you.'

'We'll be in touch with all the details as soon as we have them. We wanted your co-operation before going further with the planning stage. Thank you for your assistance, Mrs Warwick.' Brownley stood. 'If you have any questions, or second thoughts, please give me a call.' He handed her a business card. 'If for any reason I'm not there, my secretary can locate me.'

Shasta stood, never taking his eyes from Brownley.

'Good dog you have there,' Brownley said.

Jenny smiled, patting her dog as she, too, rose.

'Yes, he's a love. I feel very safe when he's around. I'll show you out, Mr Brownley.'

As the car vanished down her drive, Jenny sank to her stoop, hugging Shasta. 'So we're to become government agents. What fun!'

Shasta rested his head on her leg and sat patiently as Jenny sat on the porch, her imagination running riot. Who could be involved in this? She reviewed in her mind all the families she knew, imagination balking at anyone's involvement. Maybe it was a false alarm.

She waited over two weeks before the next call from Mr Brownley came.

'I'll come straight to the topic at hand.' He was all business. 'The cover story needs to change a little. Have you told many people yet?'

'Actually, I only mentioned to my parents that one of Johnny's cousins might be coming this summer. They had a few questions. I'm not very good at this. I guess I need the background on this guy so I'm ready for the next set of questions.'

'Scrap the writer story, if you can, or change it. This cousin was injured in a motorcycle accident and needs time to convalesce. Fortunately he's a college professor and has the summer off. The accident occurred the day after spring break started, so he's disappointed not to be able to finish the year and take his summer vacation to Europe as he planned, but is grateful his cousin's widow will let him recuperate in the mountains. Think you can handle that one?'

'Yes, of course. When will he arrive?'

'Late next week.'

'So soon? I'd better get to town and casually drop hints around. Good cover story, Mr Brownley. No one expects an injured man to be fit and able to tackle criminals.'

There was a pause on the other end. Jenny thought she detected a trace of amusement when he spoke again. 'Yes. I see you're entering into the spirit of the adventure. A word of caution, Mrs Warwick.' His voice grew serious, 'This is not a game. The stakes are high. Men have been killed over less. If you see or hear anything suspicious, let our agent know, or call me. I appreciate your help, but I don't want anything to happen to you because of it. Am I making myself clear?'

'Yes, sir. I've no desire to be the great heroine. But I am glad to be of some help. The room will be ready. What's his name?'

There was another pause, then, 'Good grief, I don't know what we want to call him! I'll check back with you on that, we need to tally with the background we're providing. Call him Martin until or unless you hear further from me. Talk to you soon.'

As soon as Jenny hung up the receiver, she thought of a couple of other questions she should have asked. Should she call him back? No, it was only a week or so until the agent arrived; she could flesh out the story then.

Going into town, she casually mentioned the arrival of the invalid to each of the owners of the businesses she worked for. Going to the chemists, she also dropped a word in Susie Lewis's ear. Susie, while one of Jenny's best friends, was also a notorious gossip. The whole town would know the story in a couple of days.

Twice more in the next few days she ventured into town, and brought the subject up. When specific questions were asked that she didn't know the answer to, she was vague.

'You know Johnny. He was never big on family. I've heard him mention some of the cousins, but I've never met any that didn't come here to visit. We always meant to go one day.' Her sad look immediately caused a change in conversation and further answers were not required.

Returning home on Tuesday, Jenny stopped the truck in surprise in front of the house. There on her doorstep, large as life and at home with Shasta lying down beside him, sat Kyle Martin!

'What in the world are *you* doing here?' She climbed out of the truck and walked quickly up the path to the doorstep.

'I checked the back door but, since the glass has been repaired, I didn't want to push my luck by breaking it again. I've been waiting for you.' He didn't get up and when Jenny got over her initial surprise she looked him over.

His left arm was in a sling. He was leaning back against the door, looking tired and drawn. Her eyes were drawn to the duffle bag and suitcase nearby.

'Kyle,' she said warningly, 'what *are* you doing here?'

'Thought I'd come to pay you a visit. Got my present, I see.'

She glared at the dog. Shasta wagged his tail, but did not get up from his place at Kyle's side.

'A fine watch-dog you are!' she scolded. 'Don't you know a crook when you see one?'

Kyle chuckled, ruffling the fur on the dog's neck. 'He's a nice dog, I think. Do you like him?'

'Kyle, you've got to go. You can't stay here. I'm expecting someone later this week. You can't stay.'

'What a girl you are for always expecting someone! Your husband last winter, a visitor later this week.'

'I mean it, you can't stay. You'll be lucky if I don't call the police.'

'You didn't last time.'

'How do you know?'

'I know.'

'Are you on the run?' she asked suspiciously, again glancing at the luggage.

'No. I need a place to stay for a while, and I thought you could put me up.'

Her heart lurched against her ribs at the thought. Why was he so attractive? His dark hair was curly, an unruly lock falling across his forehead, his dark eyes fathomless and remote. She realised she hadn't forgotten one thing about him. It wasn't fair that rogues and crooks should be handsome. They should be as ugly as their deeds.

Frustrated that he wouldn't take no for an answer, she shook her head firmly. 'No, you can't stay!'

Slowly he struggled to his feet, pale and unsteady. Jenny bit her lip, longing to reach out and help him. She remembered him as so strong, so large, so virile. What had happened to him? Why was his arm in a sling?

'Were you in a gun fight?' she asked, suspiciously.

'Yeah. I'm going to make it, though.' He drew out his wallet, flipped it open and held it out to her. 'Read it. The joke has gone far enough. I need to lie down and you won't let me in until you know. I'm the Treasury agent Brownley sent.'

CHAPTER FOUR

Jenny was astonished!

'You're a government agent? A law enforcement officer?' Her surprise reflected in the disbelief of her voice. 'I don't believe it!'

Kyle smiled down at her, his eyes crinkling at the corners in the way she had remembered so many times. His skin was pale, however, without the healthy tan he had had last March. There were new lines around his eyes and mouth. He looked haggard and ill.

'That's me. Can we go in? I haven't been out of the hospital long, and the ride up was tiring.'

She looked at him suspiciously again. 'Let me see that ID again.' She studied it carefully; it was very like the one Stuart Brownley had had. Slowly she handed it back.

'Since when does the US government condone tricking its citizens, condone breaking and entering and . . .'

'Jenny, have a heart, I'm about all in. Can we go into this later?' Kyle leaned against the wall, his skin whiter than ever.

Jenny stepped by him to unlock the door and open it. 'Stalling for answers?' she asked.

He chuckled but made no response, reaching for his duffle bag.

'I'll bring your things, you do look all in,' Jenny said in concern. 'I made up the guest room for you—for the agent, that is. It's upstairs in the back of the house.'

'I know the way,' he murmured audaciously as he entered the house.

Leading the way, Kyle headed straight for the bedroom in question, Jenny close behind with his duffle bag.

'God, I'm so tired.' Kyle sank down on the edge of the bed.

'Lie back and rest, then,' Jenny said practically. 'I'll get your suitcase.'

When she returned with the bag, he was already asleep. Gently putting the suitcase near the dresser, she turned to watch him, see how he looked, curiosity about his injury strong. Time enough to ask about that later, though, along with a few other things! She turned and left the room.

As she worked during the afternoon, an ear cocked in case he awoke, a slow anger began. Now, as she stirred the green beans for dinner, anger flared.

How dared he not identify himself last winter? He had known she was scared, and one flick of his ID badge would have cleared everything up. And how dared he tease her along today? If he were an agent, and his identification looked like Mr Brownley's, then he should have made himself known to her instantly on both occasions. Especially last winter. There would have been no need to break into her house. He could have identified himself, and she would have let him in.

A sudden thought came to her: had he suspected her of dealing in marijuana?

She stirred vigorously. No, he just loved keeping things mysterious. He probably thought it hilarious that she didn't know he was the agent Brownley was sending. She was surprised he hadn't broken in by the window again; he'd had no compunction last winter. He probably thought it amusing to use his last name as his first when she had asked. Why hadn't she had any suspicions that he was the same man?

Now dinner. What was she to do? Carry his up to him, or call him to come to dinner? Was he even awake yet? Should she let him sleep if he wasn't?

A small twinge of guilt niggled at her. She had thought Brownley's new story a cover-up. A put-up story to fool the drug growers into thinking the agent was weak. In fact, he *was*, but not as the result of a motorcycle accident, but a gun fight!

Jenny's gentle nature winced at the thought of bullets penetrating Kyle's flesh, going into the bone and sinew of the man. The picture was too distressing to envisage. She shook her head.

What about dinner?

'Do you always attack food when you're preparing it? You have every time I've seen you cook.'

Jenny whirled around. Kyle stood in the doorway, leaning against the jamb. He looked better than at her last glimpse: at least his face had some colour in it.

'Only when I'm fixing a meal for you! I suppose you think all this is a huge joke. Fool the stupid country girl!'

'No.' He moved to the table, sat down and looked up at her, his face serious. 'I couldn't tell you last winter who I was, I didn't know who you were.

Everyone was suspect. How was I to know if you were in it, too?'

'Me?'

'We've had you checked out since. You're clean. At least,' he qualified, 'we think you are.'

'Oh, thanks a lot.' She scooped up the meal—pork chops, green beans and corn—and placed his plate before him.

'When we decided to focus on this location, I recommended your place to Brownley as a possible safe place. We checked you out, and he approached you.'

'Never telling me who he was sending.'

'He told you the name. Part of it, anyway.' Kyle smiled down at his plate. 'I did hope during the last few days that you wouldn't ask for more information. I wanted to see your face when you saw it was me.'

'I hope you were suitably rewarded.' She slammed a glass of milk down in front of him.

'What's that?'

'Milk. Invalids get milk.' Her tone indicated she was longing for an argument.

'Thank you,' he said meekly.

'Once you knew I was OK, you could have filled me in,' she said as she began to eat.

He shrugged. 'Didn't see the need at the time. Later, as I said, you didn't ask. I was just waiting.'

They ate in silence for a moment. Then, 'And the kiss?' she couldn't resist asking, though she could feel the heat steal into her cheeks.

He grinned. 'A perk of the job.'

Jenny kept her eyes on her food, slowly cutting one of the chops. Only a perk of the job! She would not show her disappointment. Let that be a lesson to you, my girl, she said silently. This man is a professional, concerned with the job at hand, so don't expect anything from him and you won't be disappointed.

Jenny again broke the silence.

'You won't get away with it.'

'With what?'

'The deception. If Nate Wilson and Jim Blain were after you last February, you can't avoid seeing them if you stay around here. What's their connection?'

'I don't know, but we can find out. Have them over and I'll meet them. If they recognise me, they'll give some sort of sign. If so, we'll have to use another plan of attack. If they don't recognise me, we can proceed with this one.'

'How badly injured are you?'

'Bad enough to keep me from doing anything for another couple of weeks. Brownley said I could get started here rather than convalesce at home. I might be able to meet some people, get my background established, get people used to me. You're going to be invaluable for this.'

He surprised her when dinner was over by offering to help with the dishes. Jenny looked at him and shook her head. He still looked pale, tired.

'I can manage. Why don't you go sit under the tree, by the side of the house? I have a chair there. I'll bring another one out, and the coffee, after I finish these.'

'OK, thanks.'

When Jenny joined him half an hour later, he had turned the chair to face the west. Shasta was lounging nearby in the deepening shadows of early evening.

'I never did thank you for my dog,' she said, setting the coffee down near him. 'I love him, he's such a good friend and I feel much safer with him here. Though I will say that at the time I thought you had some nerve, sending me a watch-dog!'

Kyle chuckled and glanced over to Shasta. 'I'm glad you like him. I thought a lot about your being alone here.' Glancing back to Jenny, he gave a wicked grin. 'And I know how easy it was for people to break in.'

She ignored the comment. 'What am I to tell people about you? I've dropped small hints during the last few weeks, but nothing concrete. I didn't have a complete story, didn't have an age, occupation, all the things people like to know. If you were really Johnny's cousin, I'd have known.' Was he married? she wanted to ask. She ought to know if Johnny's cousin was married, though why would it matter?

He frowned. 'I thought Brownley had gone over that with you.'

'First you were a writer, now a college teacher convalescing from an accident. Where are you supposed to live, where do you teach, what do you teach? There are a lot of details I don't know, and people will ask. Our stories ought to match.'

'Yes, they should. You catch on quick. Let's see. Anyone around here attend San Francisco State?'

Jenny thought a moment, trying to remember where each of the college kids she knew was going to school. It didn't ring a bell. She shook her head. 'I don't think so.'

'OK, I teach Etruscan History at San Francisco State.'

Her eyes widened. 'What do you know about Etruscan history?'

'I don't know an Etruscan from a Phoenician, but I don't think anyone else will, either. I want an obscure subject, so I don't get quizzed. If I do, whatever I make up will pass, if no one else knows about it.'

'Stay clear of Mrs Peabody. She's the town librarian and has the most amazing store of trivia ever. If anyone here knows anything about something obscure, it's her.'

'Mrs Peabody. Got it.'

'You were planning to go to Europe this summer, but got into an accident, so you're visiting with your cousin's widow until you're better.'

'Right. Big disappointment, not going to Europe, but this had advantages. I like the mountains, I've never been here before, and can report back to the rest of the family on how Johnny's widow is doing.'

Jenny was side-tracked. Was that how people saw her, as Johnny's widow? She had been happy in being his wife. But she was young and would like to go on and have a life for herself. She didn't want people to always associate her as Johnny's widow. She was Jenny Warwick, a person in her own right. Free and able to do as she pleased, not restricted and tidily classified away as someone's widow.

As she prepared for bed that night, Jenny reviewed the day's events. Her opinion of Mr Brownley's plan wasn't as high as it had been. It was one thing to pretend an agent was more feeble than was true; another matter entirely to send someone who was so incapacitated that a walk up the stairs was exhausting.

Crawling between her sheets, she thought back to the other night Kyle had spent beneath her roof. He would be no match for her in his present state, and Jenny was suddenly overwhelmed with pity for him. His temporary weakness must be frustrating for him. She longed for him to be back to his normal, robust state of health.

Not that there was anything wrong with his tongue. He had not apologised for deceiving her last winter, nor the joke on his identity this time. It wasn't fair, it occurred to her as she lay there: he knew all about her, and she knew nothing about him.

Well, her mind reasoned, he'd be here for a while, at least; she could learn something in that time.

A small warm glow spread through her. She had given up expecting to see him again, and here he was, staying with her indefinitely. It was now up to her to find out what she wanted to know.

'Let's get to the project at hand,' Kyle had said, drawing Jenny's attention. She'd tilted her head as she watched him talk, hearing his voice, mesmerised by the planes and angles of his face. She had felt a long dormant tingling within her: the start of a longing to reach out and lightly draw her fingertips along the hard, firm line of his jaw.

Her eyes had widened as she'd realised what she was doing. Clenching her fist, she drew a deep breath and looked away.

Kyle had stopped in mid-sentence and peered at her closely. 'Did you hear what I said?'

'Yes,' she had nodded, smiling a little and looking back. She would discipline her thoughts to the project. She must!

'Are you from California?' she'd asked.

His face lost all expression, and it was a long moment before he replied, 'I'm from San Francisco State College, remember? In San Francisco. I'm a cousin of Johnny's . . . Weren't all his cousins born in California?'

This was to be strictly business, and Jenny was oddly disappointed.

'What exactly are you looking for?'

'You don't need to be concerned with that. You're involvement is only to provide me with a cover. I'll do the rest.'

'How can I help if I don't know what's going on?'

'You are helping, just by letting me stay. Keep out of the rest.'

Jenny had turned at his response. She had thought she would play a little more active role.

'Have you been doing this for a long time?' She'd thought he was in his early thirties. Had he always been in law enforcement?

'Long enough.'

Jenny had glanced over at him again, and her heart had caught in her throat. He lay back against the chair, skin pale, eyes shut. She had longed again to reach out to him, to comfort him, her fingers aching to touch him. She couldn't remember ever having felt as strongly as this before. What was it about Kyle Martin?

He had tired early and retired. Jenny and Shasta had, as was their habit of late, gone for a walk down the drive towards the road. By the time they returned, Kyle's lights were off.

Jenny was in her den the next morning, doing the accounts for the chemists, when she heard his tread on the stairs. She paused and looked up, gazing out of the window, her attention focused on his step. He passed by the open door without seeing her and went to the kitchen. She returned to her accounts, only to be interrupted when Kyle came back.

'Do I get breakfast?' he asked, pausing at the door.

Jenny swivelled in her chair. 'Sure, at a reasonable time. It's after ten, am I to cook all day?' She rose, glad to see he had a little more colour in his face today.

'Sorry, what time is good for you?'

She went back to the kitchen, sorry for snapping at him, yet not ready to let him know that. Normally even-tempered, she didn't know why she was so snappish around him.

Kyle followed, and sat at the table.

'I usually eat around seven. If that's too early, let me know what you want and I'll fix it and leave it in the oven to be heated.'

'No. Seven's fine,' he said meekly.

Jenny glanced sharply at him, but his face was open, innocent.

'Lunch, if I'm home, is usually sandwiches and fruit. I like to eat dinner around seven in the evening. Unless I go out.'

'Out where?' His voice was sharper, his eyes narrowed a little.

'Visiting, out with friends.' She shrugged as she poured the beaten eggs into the pan. 'Just out. I'll let you know in advance so you can plan to fix your own meals.' She turned to him. 'You do know how to cook, I take it?'

'Sure.'

'Do you live alone when not on a case?' she asked casually as the eggs cooked.

'I have an apartment near the campus; sometimes I sublet out one room to a student during the school year.'

Jenny glanced around, a frown on her face. 'I meant *really*.'

'Jenny, one way never to make a mistake is to live the role you're playing. I'm a professor at San Francisco State and I'll stick with that cover.'

But I want to know about the real you, she screamed inside. I'm not interested in cover stories, but the real story. Sighing quietly, she dished up his breakfast and put it before him.

While Kyle ate, Jenny sat with him and had another cup of coffee. When the first hunger pangs had been satisfied, he spoke. 'As soon as I'm a little more fit, I want to start going out, meeting people. You'll know best how to take me around with the least amount of comment or curiosity on the part of your neighbours.'

'Well, there's bound to be some talk; this is a small town and you're news.'

'Let's start with my going with you when you go into town. You must go in pretty often.'

'Yes, a couple or three times a week.'

'OK. Introduce me to people you see there. Then if you're invited to a party or something, ask if you can bring me along.'

Jenny nodded. 'People will be dying to see you, of course.'

'Why?'

'Because everyone knew Johnny, and they know many of his cousins. They'll be interested in meeting another.'

'Then you had better verse me in the genealogy of the Warwick family, so I don't blow it. Once I'm feeling more fit, I want you to show me the area so I can get my bearings. Maybe we can hike, or take the dog, or whatever seems appropriate.'

'I hike a lot, so that would probably cause the least amount of comment.'

'OK, where do you go?'

'Lots of places. I like to hike down near the water, but there are other hills and trails that are appealing. Since I got Shasta, I've ventured further afield.'

'Ever see marijuana growing?'

'I told your Mr Brownley, I don't know what it looks like. I may have done, or may not.'

'I'll see we get some samples so you can look for it on your hikes.'

Jenny was quiet for a moment. While she didn't like the idea of drugs, she felt a little odd in spying on neighbours and friends, trying to uncover anyone who might be growing it in their area.

'Tell me something about the people around here, the ones you know. Anyone you might suspect?' Kyle asked.

'No. I've never thought about it before, but I wouldn't have thought any of the people I know could be involved. You're sure there's marijuana being grown around here?'

'Reasonably sure. Sure enough to have me here. Any people in town flashing money around when they shouldn't be? You know, recently come into wealth, buying expensive things with a small salary? That kind of thing?'

'No. There are a few families in town that have a lot of money but have always had it. No one has come into money in the last few years that I know of.'

'Who's the town banker?'

'Mr Bottoms. He's about a hundred and three and has been in charge of the bank as long as I can remember. He might be able to tell you if anyone is banking large sums of money.'

'Maybe, but only if the account is under their own name. If they're cautious, they won't be using this bank. Does Bottoms live in town?'

'Yes. Across the street from my mom and dad, as a matter of fact.'

'Why don't you live with them?'

'Who, my parents?'

'Yes.'

Jenny looked around her. 'This is my home. Why should I leave?'

'It must have sad memories.'

'I don't know. I was very unhappy when Johnny was killed, yet I found some solace in being in the home he'd bought for us. I wouldn't want to leave it.'

'Never?' Kyle asked softly.

'Certainly not to go back to live with my parents.' She side-stepped the question. 'I'm all grown up and on my own now.'

Kyle let his eyes roam down over her figure, brought them back up to see the flush on her face as she tossed her head, meeting the appraising look in his eyes. 'Very nicely grown up, I'd say,' he murmured provocatively.

She rose and took the dishes, trying to slow the rapid rate of her heartbeat. She was vaguely pleased by the comment, but hoped he couldn't see the blush spreading on her cheeks. Odd how she was so very conscious of a man she knew very little about.

During the days that followed, Kyle spent hours questioning Jenny about the layout of the land around Palmer, the ranches and farms, the people who owned them.

Two mornings later he brought down a topographical map of the area, and he and Jenny pored over it, Jenny drawing lines indicating ranch boundaries as best she knew them, Kyle questioning her on some of the more remote areas.

Thumbnail sketches of all the owners, of the people in town, were given by Jenny. When Kyle repeated verbatim what she'd told him, she was amazed at the amount he'd learned and could recite back.

'Do you have to have a photographic memory to be an agent?' she asked when he surprised her one time with the facts she had briefly mentioned a few days earlier.

'No, just a good memory. I don't know yet what I need to know and what I don't, so I'll try to keep it all. Once I get a line on something, I can forget about the rest of it.'

'Don't you have a line on it yet? I thought that was why you were here this summer.'

'One small clue, but it's our only lead right now. I'm here to follow up on it,' Kyle said, seeing the look on Jenny's face.

'I can't believe anyone in Palmer could be involved.'

'They may not be. On the other hand, Jenny dealers excel in being just like anyone else. They don't have shifty eyes, skulk around dark alleys, or wear trench coats. That's what makes them so hard to catch, and so successful in their trade. They're just like you or me to look at.'

Jenny shivered. 'It's spooky to think someone I know might be a drug dealer. What was the clue?'

He smiled briefly and pointed to the map.

'Who lives here?'

They were off again on the map: Jenny trying to pinpoint where people lived, where the National Forest land began. She wished he would tell her more.

The next morning, after breakfast, Kyle disappeared into his room for a while, and then reappeared, asking, 'Can I borrow your truck?'

'Can't I drive you where you want to go?'

'Don't you trust me with the truck?'

'Now, Kyle, I really don't know you very well. Are you a good driver?' She smiled over at him. She hadn't known him long, but she was growing at ease in his company, felt she'd like to know him better.

He answered her smile, his warm brown eyes alight with amusement as he loomed over her.

'I'm a very good driver, never had a ticket. Do you want me to provide references?' he replied lazily.

Jenny wasn't prepared for the way his smile caused a meltdown within her. She found it difficult to breathe. Did he have any idea the effect he was having on her?

'I suppose that if you wreck it, your Department will reimburse me.'

'Sure, but I won't wreck it.'

Jenny turned from the sink, dried her hands. 'If you want to go somewhere, I'll take you. Not because I think you'll wreck my truck, but just to let you see where things are. Wouldn't that suit you?' She was still concerned about his physical stamina. His arm was in the sling, he still rested in the afternoons. Was he up to driving the pick-up? Silly, she chided herself, those were all the *right* reasons, the *real* reason was that she wanted to spend time with him.

'OK. That'll get me the layout, then I can go out on my own and not worry about getting lost.'

Jenny called for Shasta, then went to get the truck. In only a short time they were off.

As they drove towards town, Jenny pointed out driveways, roads, houses visible from the highway, and connected names with the ones they had reviewed over the last week.

'I've been here before,' Kyle murmured, slanting an amused glance at Jenny. 'But it looked different in the snow.'

'What were you doing here last winter? Surely you didn't expect to find any plants growing in the snow?'

Kyle was silent so long that Jenny turned to glance at him.

He never answered many of her questions.

'I operate under the need-to-know principle,' he said slowly. 'I've found that's the safest way for me.'

'And I don't *need* to know, is that it?' Jenny said quickly. 'Darn it, I'm providing a cover for you. I'd think the least you could do is share some of the information with me?'

'Do you? Why?'

'To satisfy my raging curiosity!' she snapped.

Her anger was perhaps a little unreasonable, but it was a culmination of the frustration of the last few days. He'd question her for hours, yet if she asked one question all she got was an evasive response, or one designed to match the cover story.

His chuckle surprised her. She threw him a dark look and turned back to her driving. He found it funny, did he?

The light touch of his fingers against her cheek caused her breath to catch. She looked over to him again, eyes widening in question.

'Just like a woman,' he murmured mockingly. 'Ever curious.'

That response did nothing to assuage her anger. They drove in silence, reaching the edge of town before Jenny spoke again.

'How did you get up here last winter?'

'Motorcycle. I left it at the garage in Strawberry and hiked over. That blasted storm about did me in.'

Jenny smiled, remembering their first encounter. It had not been amusing at the time.

Once in Palmer, they cruised up and down the cross streets, with Jenny again pointing out the families that lived in the homes, a brief sketch of the various stores and shops.

Kyle listened attentively, nodding, asking few questions.

'There's the Sheriff's office.' She slowed down as they passed, looking over to Kyle questioningly. 'Do you want to stop in? Have you already checked in with him?'

He shook his head. 'No. Until I have more to go on, I'm strictly on my own.'

'Don't you co-operate with each other?'

'When it gets down to it, of course. Some-times——' he hesitated, glanced out the window, '—sometimes the local law is in on the take. Until we know for sure, we don't blow the gaff.'

'Bob Marshall is as honest as the day is long! The thought of him being on the take is preposterous!' Jenny protested. Didn't they trust *anyone*?

'Feisty little thing, aren't you? I hope if I ever need you that you'll come as quickly to my .de-fence. I didn't say he was on the take, only that sometimes the local law is. Standard operating pro-cedures dictate that until we scout out the situation a little more thoroughly, we don't tip our hand.'

Jenny remained quiet, but threw a quick glance at Kyle. The life of an agent was certainly a sus-picious one.

Jenny turned into a gravelled drive. Ahead was a large, rambling house, a big porch across the front. There were chairs, rockers and a swing on the porch. The front door was wide open. She stopped and looked at him.

Kyle cocked an eyebrow in question.

'This is my parents' home. I think you ought to meet them. Mom will wonder if I don't bring John-ny's cousin to see her, she knows your mother. I mean Edith Gruder, who is supposed to be your mother.'

'Right. The one with three husbands. Does your mother keep up with Edith's life?'

'I don't know. I hope not, or she'll know Edith doesn't have a son.'

'I hope not, too, for my sake.' Kyle opened his door and stepped out.

As they entered the spacious house, Jenny called out.

'In the back, darling. Come on through,' her mother called back.

When they reached the back-yard, they found Jenny's mother weeding one of the flower-beds bordering the house. She rocked back on her heels, smiling at her daughter. Seeing Kyle, she hastened to her feet, wiping her hands on the small towel hanging from her waist as she came to greet them.

Kyle knew what Jenny would look like in twenty years. Peggy O'Neil was still trim and pretty. Her light brown hair had little grey showing in it, her eyes still sparkled and her smile was warm in its welcome.

'Mom, I'd like you to meet Kyle Martin. He's a cousin of Johnny's. Kyle, this is my mother, Peggy O'Neil.'

'How do you do, Mrs O'Neil? I'm happy to meet you.'

'Kyle Martin. Which cousin are you?'

'My mother is Johnny's Aunt Edith.'

A large smile broke across Peggy's face. 'Edith Warwick, she was always my favourite, as girls. We were great friends then. Is she happy? I can't help thinking she must be, for all she marries all the time. Which husband is your father?'

'Number two.' Kyle and Jenny had worked that out already.

'I haven't seen or talked to Edith in years and years. Give her my best next time you see her. Tell her to come visit.'

'I'll do that.'

Jenny bit her lip to keep from laughing. Kyle looked so sincere! She felt she had to change the topic.

'Kyle had an accident, on his motorcycle. He wanted a place to convalesce, so he's staying with me a while.'

Her mother looked at Jenny, then back to Kyle, a small frown on her face. 'Alone?'

'Well, hardly, Mom. Shasta's with us, too.' Jenny turned away. She could just imagine the thoughts her mother would soon have. She felt it was high time Jenny started looking for another husband. As if one went looking for a husband as one shopped for a car! Jenny was uncertain if she wanted to remarry. She had been so happy with Johnny. Wouldn't there be some disloyalty if she found happiness with someone else? Maybe not, but she wanted to be the one to decide, rather than do it because her mother thought it a good idea.

If her mother started on that trend with Kyle, Jenny would leave, just get up and walk away. Mothers could be trying at times!

'Won't you sit down, Kyle? You don't mind if I call you that? I'm practically an aunt, too, by marriage. Would you like some lemonade?'

'Thank you, that would sure be good, if it's not too much trouble.' Kyle smiled at her and moved to sit in one of the outside chairs. Jenny looked at him closely; he was looking just a trifle white around his temples. Maybe the outing was too soon. How ill was he?

'I'll get it, Mom. Be right back.'

Just as she went into the kitchen, she heard her mother ask, 'Are you a married man, Kyle?'

CHAPTER FIVE

JENNY turned, wanting to hear the answer to that question. She met Kyle's amused glance, blushed and continued to the kitchen. As she got the glasses and ice for the lemonade, she fumed at the timing of her mother's question. Now she wouldn't know! And she couldn't ask her mother, she should already know the answer to that question.

Dreaming idly, she wondered what it would be like to be married to Kyle Martin. Exciting was the first thought to spring to mind. He practically radiated sex appeal, was fun to be with, and had a genuine concern for other people. Yet there was much he refused to reveal—would he be more open with his wife? Or would he stick with his need-to-know philosophy? Then there was the worry of his job. The accident proved it wasn't always a safe and secure job. What would it be like to be married to Kyle? Was he already married?

Filling the glasses, she wondered if Kyle would volunteer that information, so if she was asked by someone else, her answer would match what her mother knew. She would ask him herself. She should know, so that they could have their stories straight.

Carrying the tray carefully outside, Jenny reflected that no matter what answer Kyle had given, it was not necessarily true. He would answer as

Johnny's cousin, as it suited his cover for this assignment.

They did not linger after they'd finished the refreshing beverage. Kyle still wanted to see more, and Jenny knew her mother wanted to finish her weeding. It was so rare that she was in the mood to do weeding that Peggy disliked being distracted from it.

Back in the truck, they moved on, going east of the town.

'Are you sure you should be doing so much, so soon after getting out of the hospital?'

'I'm doing my damnedest to get fit as quickly as I can. It's so slow sometimes.' His voice was hoarse with impatience.

'Some things you just can't rush,' she said reasonably.

'This is important, though. I can't languish around for ever.'

'You're hardly doing that. First, it's not *for ever*; I think you're up much too early. Now you're out and about and, if I know you—and I'm starting to—you're probably up to something.'

'Not till I've seen the doctor again. I'm not foolish enough to rush in where permanent damage might be the result.'

'I'm surprised to hear that.' He seemed so masculine, so macho. Jenny was a little surprised he was admitting to any limitation. When was he seeing a doctor? She asked him.

'I need to go to Sacramento next week.'

'Dr Bradley in town could see you.'

'Sure, and there goes the motorcycle story. Bullet wounds are somewhat distinctive,' he remarked drily.

Jenny blushed at his tone. She had not thought of that. 'I can take you down to Sacto, if you like.' A thought struck her. 'How else would you get there?'

'Brownley.'

Of course. Brownley had brought him to Jenny's. Kyle had no car; he needed some means to get around.

'Is he around here?'

'No, he's in Sacramento.'

'Well, the offer stands.'

Jenny resumed her narrative on the people and their residences, the boundaries of the ranches as they drove east. Circling around, she returned home in the early afternoon.

The telephone was ringing when they reached home. Jenny ran to answer it, breathless by the time she reached it.

'Hello, Jenny?' The voice was vaguely familiar.

'Yes.'

'George Carlisle here. I've been out of town on business. Sorry I haven't called for a while.'

'George, how nice to hear from you.' Jenny had gone out with him a couple of times since running into him in the early spring. He was older than she, moved in a different circle from her, but he was a pleasant companion. He took her to different places, always conscious of what might please her.

'I'm giving a barbecue soon, and I wanted to make sure you could come. Probably the Saturday after next.'

'Yes, I'd love to. Can I bring anything?'

'A salad? A cake? Whatever you feel like. There'll be about fifty guests, I expect everyone will bring something. I'm providing the beef and chicken for the barbecue.'

Kyle reached the hall as Jenny listened to George, reminding her of another question.

'George, one of Johnny's cousins is staying with me. Can I bring him, too?'

'Sure, the more the merrier. I didn't know you had house guests.'

'Just Kyle. Why don't you come for dinner tomorrow night? You can meet him then.'

'Sounds like a fine idea.'

'Come about seven.'

'Good. See you then.'

Kyle stood and watched Jenny as she hung up the phone. She turned a bright face to him.

'There! Your first social occasion, at George Carlisle's. He's one of the ranchers from around here, we saw his ranch this morning. He's having a barbecue in a week or so, and invited us. You can meet lots of people there, establish your background. Maybe get asked around.'

'Who's George Carlisle?'

'A rancher—I just said.'

'A special friend?'

'Well,' Jenny was reluctant to admit to that, 'we've gone out a few times since this spring. He's nice.'

Kyle turned away and began to climb the stairs. 'Nice is no threat,' he murmured as he went up. 'I'll be down for dinner.'

'Don't you want lunch?'

'No. I want to lie down.' He paused and looked over the banister, down at her. 'Thanks for the lift and the tour.'

As Jenny prepared for bed that night, she remembered their brief conversation that afternoon, about the gunshot wounds. She had not let herself dwell on it before, but now she let her imagination have full rein. How awful it must have been! She could envision the shock, the pain Kyle must have felt. Had he received immediate attention? Had he been with a partner, or alone with the suspect? She closed her eyes tightly to black out the picture.

She could also see how impatient he was with the time it was taking to heal. He was a man of action, wanting to move, react. To wait patiently for a healing process in which he played very little part must be very annoying and taxing for him. She wondered if there was any permanent damage. Would he be completely well soon?

She longed to ask him more about it, but didn't know him well enough to try. She was afraid to have him scoff at her if she asked.

The next evening Jenny took care to dress up for dinner. It was the first time George had been to her house, and she wanted it to be special, to show her appreciation of the enjoyable evenings they had spent together over the last few months. She took pains with dinner, freshened the house and put a bouquet of late spring flowers in the dining-room. The evenings were cool and pleasant, so they could have their coffee on the lawn.

The blue and white sundress she wore was simple, yet flattering to her figure. It showed off the light tan she had already acquired. She didn't often wear dresses but liked to, when appropriate. Jenny felt very feminine in the soft skirt and the fitted bodice. She brushed her hair until the highlights shone. Putting her make-up on sparingly, she was ready.

Kyle was already downstairs when Jenny drifted down the stairs. He watched her descent, his expression unreadable.

Jenny feasted her eyes on him, his pale shirt crisp and fresh, showing off the breadth of his shoulders, the dark brown cords moulding the length of his long legs. He was rested and relaxed, the colour back in his face, his eyes bold and assessing.

Jenny felt the colour steal into her cheeks, but could do nothing to stop it. She felt his gaze as a caress and the trembling deep within her threatened to spill out to her knees and hands.

'You look lovely,' Kyle said softly as she reached the front hall.

'Thank you.' Shyly she walked over to him, breathlessly drawing near him. Would he move to let her pass? They could wait for George in the living-room.

'All dressed up for the neighbour, eh?'

Jenny blinked. 'Sure, he's a good friend and I want him to enjoy himself tonight.'

'Shall I excuse myself after dinner so you can enjoy yourself?'

She understood the hidden meaning and shook her head. If she wanted something like that, it wouldn't be with George Carlisle.

'No need,' she replied stiffly, staring up into his face. The fine lines around his eyes were paler than his tanned cheeks, the lips full and sensuous, his

dark eyes fathomless pools in which she could fall
and lose herself for ever.

'Jenny——' His voice was low, husky as he gently
trailed his knuckles down her heated cheek, across
her jaw-line, down her throat. 'If you continue to
look at me like that, your friend's going to miss
dinner.'

Jenny swayed towards Kyle, her mind racing,
tumbling with visions of what might happen. The
vision vanished as she heard the throaty growl of
George's Porsche on the gravelled drive.

With a sigh—hers or his?—she stepped back and
went to the door to greet her guest.

Surprised by a large bouquet of roses, she was
pink and flustered as she made the introductions.

Under the pretence of smelling the fragrant blos-
soms, she studied the two men. They were totally
different, each distinguished in his own right. Kyle
was taller, broader, much more rugged. His dark,
unruly hair, his brown eyes, narrowed now, his
tanned skin, all blending together gave him a rakish appearance, an earthy, robust stance. Clearly a
man of action.

George would have been at home at a corporate
board meeting. He was slim, dapper, with a small
moustache covering his top lip. His eyes were rather
nondescript—hazel, Jenny thought. He had an aura
of fastidiousness around him in contrast to Kyle's
earthiness.

She smiled at them both.

'I'll just put these in water. Why don't you go on
into the living-room? I'll join you in just a moment.'

The men moved to the room, each watching the other. Kyle gave way first, seeking a chair near the sofa, from where he could see the whole room. No matter where George chose to sit, Kyle could easily converse with him. George chose the sofa.

Jenny, coming in with drinks, paused only a moment before joining George on the sofa.

'I know what Kyle likes.' She handed him his glass. 'And, George, I remembered what you always ordered when we ate out—gin and tonic. OK?'

'Fine, thank you, my dear.' George raised his glass in silent toast and sipped.

Jenny was flustered. He had never called her 'dear' before; it was almost like he was staking a claim. Why tonight, of all nights? She threw a quick glance at Kyle. He was looking at his drink. Had he heard? Suddenly he looked up, catching her gaze. His sardonic expression showed he had.

'Jenny said you were one of Johnny's cousins. Don't believe we've met before, and yet I thought I knew most of the Warwicks.' George settled back, his demeanour calm and thoughtful.

'Edith's son,' Jenny murmured, looking at her glass, her emotions whirling. She had not thought of George as anything other than a friend. Surely that was all he saw her as . . .

'I haven't visited here in—oh, years and years. Since I was a kid,' Kyle said lazily. 'Wasn't planning on it this summer, either, but since I crashed my bike, I thought why not? Now that I've met Jenny, I'm glad it happened.'

Jenny jerked her head up at this, had she heard right?

'An accident on a motorcycle?' George was polite.

'Yeah. Broken collarbone. I'll be fine in a few weeks, but in the meantime, it put paid to my plans to visit Europe this summer.'

The conversation centred on Kyle as he and Jenny slowly unfolded the story they had concocted. George was polite, probing. Kyle answered all questions in a casual, careless manner, more than once alluding to a growing relationship between him and his cousin's widow. Jenny grew more and more nervous as the questions went on, glaring at Kyle, trying to catch his eyes to squelch the trend of the conversation. He ignored her. Was this his idea of a joke?

Just wait until she had him alone! She'd set him on his ear! What did he think he was doing? As Kyle grew more and more expansive, George grew more and more reserved. Jenny felt guilty about leading him on. He was a nice man, and did not deserve the story Kyle was giving him.

'I'll just check on dinner, shall I?' Unable to stand the conversation any longer, she jumped up and hurried into the kitchen. Her hands were shaking slightly.

Was George always so inquisitive? Jenny didn't know him well enough to know if he were or not. The town thrived on gossip, yet she hadn't thought George the type to spread it. He was asking a lot of questions tonight, however.

Quickly she dished up the meal: fried chicken she had prepared earlier, vegetables, potato cakes, iced tea to drink. She had prepared a blueberry tart for dessert. Surely the conversation would change at dinner?

The meal passed pleasantly, much to her relief. The evening was beginning to wear on her. Dessert and coffee they took on the lawn, the evening cool but not unpleasant. Shasta joined them when they came outside, keeping close to Jenny's side.

'Odd how she got that dog, don't you think?' George said as he began his second cup of coffee.

'I don't believe I know how she got it,' Kyle said. 'Buy it in a pet shop?'

'No, mysteriously the dog arrived one day, fully trained.'

'Not so mysterious,' Jenny protested. 'A...a friend sent him.'

'But why, and why a trained German Shepherd? We haven't had a wild attacker running amok, so why the trained dog?'

'Why not?' Jenny said lightly, her eyes seeking Kyle's.'

'He's a friendly thing,' Kyle said, snapping his fingers. Shasta lumbered up and went to Kyle, his tail wagging. Kyle fondled his ears.

'To you, maybe. I keep my distance around him,' George said. 'Planning to stay the entire summer here, Kyle?'

'If Jenny doesn't get too tired of having me around. By the time I'm fit again, it will be far too late to get to Europe. School starts in September, so I'll just hang around till then, I guess.'

Jenny sipped her coffee to hide her smile. Kyle sounded so unsure, so vague. Totally unlike the real Kyle. Was he expecting George to talk about the cousin visiting Jenny, to spread the tale of his weakness, his indecisiveness? If it would lull people, it would be worth it. But George was not the type to chat casually about his neighbours and their affairs. Kyle picked the wrong man to spread the story if he thought George would do it.

When George took his leave, he asked Jenny to walk him to his car. They talked in low tones, and then he took her hand.

'I've enjoyed myself, Jenny. In a way, I'm sorry Kyle is here, but he's a pleasant enough fellow. Practically one of the family, I see, being Johnny's cousin and all. Though maybe in the near future, you and I could go out to dinner without him.'

Jenny smiled. 'I'd like that.' Anything to avoid another evening like tonight.

'I'll see you at the barbecue.' He gave her hand an extra squeeze and turned to get into his car.

Jenny watched as he drove off and wandered slowly back to where Kyle was still sitting, next to Shasta.

'Just how close are you two?' Kyle asked as she stacked the cups and saucers.

'Not that it's any of your business,' she said coolly, 'but we're just friends. Actually George is the older brother of a guy I went to school with. We ran into each other a few months ago and have gone out once or twice.'

'He's too old for you, too pedantic.'

'I'll pick my own friends, thank you,' she said, turning.

She gathered everything up and went to the kitchen. Kyle rose and followed her in, leaning against the counter as she washed and wiped the last of the dishes. As she was drying her hands on the towel, he reached out and gently took her wrist, drawing her over to him, against him, his good arm going around her back as he bent his head to kiss her.

His lips were warm and firm against Jenny's, seductive and persuasive as he moved them gently against her, and she found herself slowly opening her mouth for a deeper kiss. His tongue traced the soft inner skin of her lip, moved to her teeth, then thrust boldly into the moist sweetness, teasing her tongue, inviting it to invade his mouth. His touch was arousing, exciting, enticing.

Jenny felt rocked to her heels. The warm feel of Kyle's body was a delight, his arm strong, his mouth wreaking sweet havoc on hers, his chest solid against the softness of her breasts. She stood quietly for a moment, then returned the kiss with great enthusiasm. Remembering suddenly the last kiss they had shared, she stopped, drew back.

'Another perk, Kyle?'

His arm dropped, as his eyes took on a wicked glint. 'Of course!'

'Brownley didn't explain that part of the job,' she retorted.

He roared with laughter, his face open with the delight her comment caused, his eyes warm with amusement. He reached over to her again, taking her chin, and dropping a light kiss on her mouth. And another, rubbing his lips against hers.

'I'll be sure and tell him of his omission next time I see him. George is not the man for you.'

Who is? she wanted to ask. Instead, Jenny shrugged. 'I don't think he wants to be.' Though some of his comments tonight had made her wonder. 'He's just being neighbourly. I think you'll like his place. It's modern and trendy, without being too outlandish.'

'You should be around traditional things, not chrome and glass.'

Jenny frowned. Did he think she was not modern? Was she old-fashioned? She opened her mouth to deny the charge, when Kyle tilted her head again, his lips brushing lightly against hers.

Jenny's heart began a slow, heavy beat as the tingling touch of his mouth brought her awake, alert, uncertain.

'Dinner was nice.' He kissed her again, his lips warm and firm. 'Dessert was nice.' Again the warm pressure. 'You're nice.'

His mouth covered hers, moving against her lips, the moist tip of his tongue tantalising the softness of her lips. Involuntarily, Jenny relaxed and opened her mouth a little, caught up in the sweetness of his touch. She held her breath as he ran his tongue against the soft fleshy inner lip, against her pearly teeth, around her lips again. She exhaled reluctantly when Kyle raised his head. Slowly she opened her eyes, blinking in the brightness of the light.

Kyle's fingers moved to her throat, caressing softly, then to her shoulders.

'Goodnight, Jenny, sleep well.'

She nodded, afraid to trust her voice, then turned and hastened up the stairs, her thoughts in turmoil.

She didn't even try for coherent order until she was beneath her sheets.

Lying in the still night, she reviewed the evening: George's surprising endearment, Kyle's allusions. Kyle's goodnight kisses. His touch was so exciting, his casual approach hard to figure out. Was he really just whiling away the time while on assignment, or was there anything more to his actions?

She turned over, trying for sleep, only to have new thoughts spring to the front of her mind. Wishing she had heard the answer to her mother's question, she wondered whether, even if she had, it would tell her anything? If his cover dictated he not be married, that was what he'd say, no matter if it was true or not.

But a married man wouldn't be kissing a woman he hardly knew, would he? Even as a perk?

Why not? her mind jeered. He probably considered it a light dalliance, a mild flirtation—as he had said, only a perk of the job. Jenny didn't like the thought, yet it persisted. She knew she had lived a rather sheltered, old-fashioned life. Johnny had been her first and only lover. He had been faithful to her and she to him since they started dating. But in the 1980s it was just as common to have open marriages, for partners to have affairs with others to keep the marriage fresh.

What would Johnny think if he could see her tonight? She felt disloyal and guilty at enjoying Kyle's kiss. She turned over on her back, gazing into the inky darkness. Rationally, she knew she was free to do what she wished. Johnny was gone, never to come back. Still, she had loved him all her life, never looked at another man. Until now.

Kyle was fascinating, intriguing. But not for her, if he believed in casual sex, casual relationships.

Jenny made a face in distaste. A casual relationship would never work for her, nor for anyone she would want to marry again, should she ever wish to do so. But did Kyle approach things that way?

She remembered how he had ruthlessly broken into her house last winter, with no thought of her fright, or of any inconvenience it might have brought her. Was he equally ruthless in his own private life? Did he subjugate everything to the job, taking his pleasures where he could find them, moving on when the next job came up? Or did he have a loving family in the background to which he returned after each assignment. Would he tell her if she asked?

On this, Jenny fell asleep.

Jenny's emotions were under control by breakfast the next morning. She greeted Kyle with a sunny smile.

'You don't have your sling on,' she noticed as she dished up his eggs.

'I'm trying without it. This convalescing takes too long.'

'Don't stop bullets any more.' She sat down across from him and watched as he began to eat.

He was still holding his left arm stiffly, not moving it even though it was free of the sling. Once, he reached for the salt with it, grimacing as he drew it back, his face paling.

'Why do men have to be so macho?' she jeered softly. 'Don't rush it. You could slow the healing, instead of hastening it.' She pushed the salt across the table.

'Yes, Mama,' he replied.

Jenny laughed aloud. 'When do you see your doctor again?'

'Later this week. Still want to drive me to Sacramento?'

'Instead of Brownley?'

'It would save him a trip. I'll buy you lunch.'

'Oh, boy, take the lady out for a treat to the big city!'

'We can discuss the situation here more fully.'

'Good grief, you've picked my brain clean. I don't think there is anything else to learn about the citizens of Palmer. But I'll take you up on lunch.'

Two days later they drove south on US 50 into the capital city. Jenny followed the directions Kyle gave, and soon parked in front of the large medical centre near downtown.

'Want to come with me and hold my hand?' he asked as he opened the door. He was wearing the sling for the trip, though he had not worn it much during the last few days. He had regained his colour and looked more robust and fit.

Jenny smiled and shook her head. 'I'll wait here. There are benches under the trees and the day is nice. Besides, anyone less in need of having their hand held, I'll never meet.'

CHAPTER SIX

JENNY was sitting beneath one of the large oak trees shading the lawn of the medical centre when Kyle came across the grass to her. The sling was gone. His left hand was tucked into the pocket of his tight jeans, held immobile, yet without the sling.

Jenny noticed how the worn jeans outlined his body, fit snugly and left little to the imagination. His hand only made them tighter. She drew her eyes away with effort.

Kyle grinned at Jenny as she rose to meet him.

'All set?' she asked.

'Yep. Almost fit. No more sling. I don't have to come back, either, unless I have problems.'

She fell into step with him as they walked back to the truck. 'But you still have to take it easy for a while?' she guessed.

'Ummm...there was some mention of that, but you know doctors. Want to eat at Shiloh's? It overlooks the American River.'

'Sounds fine.'

They ate on the wooden deck at the back of the popular riverside restaurant, overlooking the wide, placid river. The day was warm, the air soft and scented with the flowering lilacs in nearby profusion.

When lunch was over, Kyle directed Jenny to a high-rise office block.

'I need to check in at the office, make a few calls. Want to see the office?'

'Sure, I always wanted to see how government agents worked.'

Kyle chuckled at her comment, but made no reply.

Parking in the multi-storey garage, Jenny followed him into the glass and steel office building, where they were whisked to the tenth floor. The office reminded Jenny of newspaper rooms she had seen in old movies. There was a sea of desks in the centre of the open space, enclosed offices around the perimeter. Men were clustered here and there in small groups; some on the phones at their desks.

As they walked in and threaded their way through the desks, Kyle was greeted by two or three of the men at their desks.

'How are you doing?' one man called.

'Fit and ready for action?' laughed another.

'Who's your friend?' Two men walking by paused and smiled at Jenny. She smiled back shyly. Kyle just nodded, waved and kept walking. When he reached the far side, he paused near a door.

'There's a chair, have a seat. When I've made my calls, I'll show you around and introduce you to one or two of the more acceptable of my fellow workers.'

Jenny smiled and sat where indicated while Kyle disappeared into the office, closing the door. She didn't have to wait for his introduction. In only a couple of minutes Stuart Brownley came out of another office, pausing in surprise when he saw Jenny, and came over to speak to her.

'Hello, Mrs Warwick! Nice to see you again. What are you doing here? Waiting to see me?' He looked just as he had the day he had visited Jenny. She wondered briefly if it were the same suit, or if all his suits were brown.

'Hello, Mr Brownley. I came with Kyle Martin. He's making some phone calls and I'm just waiting for him. I drove him in to the doctors.'

'Of course. I would have sent a car for him, but it was nice of you to drive him.'

Jenny blinked at the comment. Had she missed something along the way? Kyle hadn't presented it quite that way.

'It wasn't any trouble. Actually, I got a nice lunch out of it, and now I'm seeing how secret agents really work.'

He laughed and glanced around the large floor, as if seeing it anew.

'Well, it's probably disappointing, no trench coats or hats pulled down over faces. Come on, I'll show you around. Kyle could be tied up for a while.'

Jenny went, and was introduced to many of the men at the desks. They ranged in age from early twenties to two who had to be in their sixties. There was a certain air about them all that marked them as individuals in the same line of work: a certain toughness, alertness, a certain wariness.

One or two knew the connection between Jenny and Kyle Martin, but she was puzzled by a few comments.

'No wonder Kyle picked that assignment!'

'Now I know why Kyle took this one on!'

She asked questions, was shown some of the equipment used for field surveys, and visited a small informal drug museum, which displayed different illegal drugs in various stages.

Kyle found them there.

'Wondered where you'd wandered off to, Jenny. Hello, Stuart.'

'Kyle. How are things going?'

'Slowly. I have some background, a couple of leads, maybe. I can start field work soon as I build up some stamina.'

'I can get you some help, if you like,' Brownley said.

'Thanks. I'll call when I need it. If anyone else becomes involved at this stage, it'll give the show away. Jenny's been a big help.'

'I have?' She was surprised. She still didn't believe there *was* drug activity in Palmer, and she wondered what she might have said to lead Kyle to believe there was, or that anyone she knew would be involved. What was that clue they were following up on?

'Yes, both for the cover, and the background you've given. Ready?'

'Yes. Thank you, Mr Brownley. I enjoyed the tour.'

'My pleasure, Mrs Warwick. Come again. Kyle, I'll be talking to you.'

'Right.'

Jenny's head was buzzing as she drove back to Palmer. She was trying to assimilate all she had just seen. The maps of the state where large acres of marijuana cultivation were known or suspected, the many different methods people used to transport the drugs, the resale value of the different kinds.

She knew drug abuse and illegal use were prevalent, but she had never realised to what extent.

Kyle was silent on the ride, watching the passing scenery from the window. Jenny didn't try to talk, caught up in her own thoughts. Once or twice she glanced over, but his look was shuttered, remote, and she didn't say anything.

Kyle's taciturn manner continued for the rest of the day. He went to the den and sat at her desk when they returned, working on the maps, checking notes he had made of the people and locals she had described to him.

At dinner, he continued to be silent. Twice Jenny looked up to find his eyes on her. Silently watching her, speculatively.

'Do I have something on my face?' she asked nervously, for the second time.

'No. I'm thinking of moving on, Jenny.'

Her heart plummeted. Slowly, carefully, she lowered her fork so her fingers didn't rattle it against her plate. She had difficulty getting her breath.

'Why?'

'Something Stuart said today hit home. Drug dealers are ruthless. I don't want anything to happen to you as a result of this. We'll set up headquarters somewhere else around here, operate from there. I shouldn't have come here, it was a mistake.'

'But your cover... I thought you needed an unobtrusive way to get to know people, to gather your evidence. I thought you needed me to provide you with that cover. It seems to be working.'

'Fine, so far. But it'll be safer if I move on.'

'Nobody suspects.'

'Jenny, I've not been doing all I will be doing from now on. That shooting set me back. Now I'm better I'll be investigating for all I'm worth, to get this area cleared again. To find and arrest any perpetrators. It could get messy.'

Jenny searched his face, feeling she was sitting across from a stranger. The same stranger who had invaded her home last winter. Gone was the gentle look on Kyle's face, the tired, ill look he had had when he had first returned. Now he looked like the hardened professional he was. There was no room for emotion or sentimentality in the man opposite her. The angles of his face seemed harder, his eyes narrowed as he watched her, the leashed energy—evident last winter—was back.

'You chose me,' she said quietly, but firmly. She was trembling a little, wondering briefly where the words were coming from. 'You and Brownley and all the government men involved in this. Chose me to be your cover, to provide you with all the information I could about this area. I didn't ask to get into this, you *chose* me. Now, it's too late, you can't leave.'

'Why not?' he challenged.

'Because I'd blow your cover sky high! I'd tell the world what you're doing, and how do you think that would help your chances of finding the guys?' she threw out recklessly.

'That's childish. It would slow me down, but it wouldn't change anything in the long run.' He pushed back from the table, throwing his napkin down. As he started down the hall, Jenny scrambled after him.

'I'll call the Sheriff and tell him you're the man who broke in last winter.'

Her voice stopped him. Slowly Kyle turned and looked at her. Jenny paused and backed up until she was against the wall. She didn't like the look in his face. Had she pushed him too far? Nervously she licked her lips.

'Did you report the break-in?'

'Yes,' she whispered.

He loomed over her, backing her further against the wall, coming so close that his body imprisoned her, pressing her back further. His right arm came up near her face as he leaned his weight on it.

'Liar,' he said pleasantly. 'Just how do you plan to explain my staying here over the last few weeks, meeting your parents, your friends? Lover's quarrel gotten out of hand?'

He leaned down and took her lips, his hard and demanding as his body pressed against her. Jenny's palms pushed against the wall in a desperate effort to resist encircling his neck, in holding him to her with all the longing that was in her. As his tongue thrust into her mouth, she gave a small moan.

He meant to punish, but to Jenny it was a delight. Raking her teeth with his moist tongue, he plunged deep into her soft mouth, wreaking havoc with her senses, her body igniting with the flame he lit, the heat rising as he continued his sweet assault.

The hard wall of his chest pressed against her soft breasts, pushing her as if he wanted to send her through the wall. The long, hard length of his thighs imprisoned her legs, and as hot need for him inflamed her, she felt his desire for her rise, press against her.

Unable to stop herself any longer, her arms rose to encircle his neck, to respond to his kiss, to mould her body to his as still he kissed her.

It went on and on: slowly they swayed as the tempo of their heartbeats increased in unison, as the heat rose and passion and desire swamped them.

Now she knew why she hadn't wanted him to leave, why she'd issued her threat.

Kyle pulled his mouth away to seek the soft pulse at the base of her throat, to trail hot kisses along the satiny skin of her neck and shoulder. His hot lips were raining light caresses across her cheeks, her eyes, her forehead, and back to claim the sweet delight of her mouth.

'I want you so damn much, Jenny. Sleep with me tonight,' he said in a throaty voice against her mouth. His breathing was heavy, hot against her fevered skin.

Jenny drew back in shocked surprise, speechless for a moment.

'I can't,' she whispered back, closing her eyes against the desire flooding through her, the longing for fulfilment of the proof of his desire.

'Why not?' Sweet, hot kisses punctuated his speech. 'We're of age....I won't hurt you...you're not a virgin....there's no one to get hurt.'

Only me, she protested, easing herself back a little, regret evident in her eyes as she opened them and looked at him. She shook her head gently.

'I...no, I won't, Kyle.'

'Come on, Jenny. Why not? Surely that kiss shows you desire me. It could be so good!'

'Let me go! Just five minutes ago you were telling me you're leaving, and now you want me to sleep with you? What for, so you have something to remember me by?' She dragged up what strength she could muster and pushed against him. It was like pushing against a mountain. 'Let me go!'

'No.' He tightened his grip. 'I want you, and you want me, or else you're the best little actress I've ever come across. So what game are you playing now?'

She blushed at his remark. She did want him, and if there had been anything more to it than lust, she wouldn't wait another second. She would love to lie in a soft bed with him, have his lips learn her while she learned him, to share love with this hard man. But he spoke no word of love. Just want, desire.

'No game, Kyle, let me go. Let me go!'

She began to struggle, pushing against him, balling her hand into a fist and lashing out, frantic to get free, connecting with his shoulder. He dropped her and staggered back against the wall, his face suddenly ashen.

'Oh, Kyle, I'm so sorry. Your shoulder—I forgot. I didn't mean to hurt you. I'm so sorry!' Contrite, Jenny reached out to hold his arm. He had seemed so much back to normal, so alive and well, that she had forgotten he really wasn't.

'I'm sorry.' She wouldn't have hurt him for anything, she had only wanted to be released.

'At least you've made your point,' he said shakily. Giving a deep sigh, he opened his eyes, looking down at her. 'You pack quite a wallop. Consider joining up, if you get tired of living up here.' He stood and walked slowly down the hall.

Jenny watched him go, torn with conflict. She wished she had grasped what he had offered; one night of glorious love might be worth all the heartache when he left. Would she regret turning him down? No, it was right.

Right be damned! she thought, going back to the kitchen to do the dishes. She felt as if she had just made a momentous decision, and a wrong one.

Jenny was still suffering from vain regrets when she awoke the next morning. She had tossed and turned during the long night, wishing things had been different. Wishing she had responded differently. Slowly the thought came to her: if she was offered the chance again, she wouldn't turn it down. Could she get Kyle to stay? Could she have him make the offer again?

Sure, if he really wanted her. She would find a way. She'd start this morning, at breakfast. With that thought in mind, she went downstairs to prepare the meal.

Kyle wasn't in the house.

Jenny called him, looked in the den, the kitchen. She glanced outside, but there was no sign of him. With her heart in her throat, she slowly went back upstairs and into his room. Had he gone, left as he said he was going to do? His clothes were still in the wardrobe, and she sagged against the door in relief. Wherever he was, he would be back.

Spending the morning doing the laundry, Jenny stripped the beds, emptied the linen basket and worked at her desk between loads as the washer did its work. Once the clothes and sheets were finished, she sorted, folded, and went to put the things away. Making her bed, she quickly put away her clothes.

She went into Kyle's room. It took only a few minutes to make the bed. She then turned to the dresser to put away his clothes. The top drawer opened easily beneath her fingers. Her breath caught. There, on top of a couple of handkerchiefs, was a gun.

She stared at it for a long minute. She frowned, picturing it in his hand: Kyle confronting another armed man. A gunshot. She shook her head at the picture. He had already been shot once, what if he were again, more critically next time? Fear for his very life coursed through her as she envisaged the danger he faced. She couldn't stand it if he were killed!

Ignoring the gun, she put away his things. Slamming shut the last drawer, she fled the room, trying to flee the thoughts and pictures her mind played.

The phone rang, interrupting her musing. She hurried to answer it. It was one of the men she had met in Sacramento, Jason Sperry.

'Have Kyle call me when he gets back,' he said when Jenny told him Kyle wasn't in.

'Call you there?'

'Yes. I have the information he requested yesterday.'

'I don't know when he'll be back.'

'If he doesn't reach me here, he has my home phone number. I'll take the stuff with me.'

'I'll tell him when he comes in.'

The day dragged by. Jenny tried her best to keep herself busy with work and household chores. Time and time again, however, her gaze was drawn outside. She searched from each window, looking for Kyle. Where had he gone? He was coming back, wasn't he? He had talked about leaving, but he wouldn't leave this way. Anyway, she told herself, his clothes were still all upstairs.

Shasta patiently padded at Jenny's side as she wandered restlessly through the house. As the afternoon waned, Jenny looked at her dog.

'Are you a tracker? If you were a bloodhound, you could find him for me.'

Shasta cocked his head, his tail slowly thumping on the floor. Suddenly, he leaped to his feet and ran to the door, his tail wagging furiously.

Kyle opened it and calmly walked in.

Jenny's heart skipped a beat, then began a slow heavy pounding.

'Hi,' she smiled, swallowing the nervous flutter. 'Been sleuthing?' The worry of earlier was suddenly gone; he hadn't left!

He grinned back at her, nodding. 'Yes, and I'm beat. Do I have time to take a shower before dinner?'

'Sure.'

Once she heard the water running, Jenny slipped up to her room to freshen her make-up, brush her hair and touch just a little of her perfume to her neck, ears, between her breasts. Leaving the top three buttons of her shirt unfastened, she smiled saucily in the mirror, before turning to return to the kitchen.

When Kyle came in, he sat at his usual place. Jenny watched, her eyes feasting on him: on the still damp, dark hair springing up from his forehead, his wide shoulders, the colour now back in his face. His brown eyes were wary, watchful as he took his seat. The dark shirt and tight jeans emphasised his athletic build, his fitness. To look at him, it didn't seem possible he had been so seriously injured only a few weeks ago.

Jenny brought his dinner, leaning over to place his plate on the table, her arm casually brushing his shoulder. She went for iced tea, placing it near him, the perfume filling his nostrils as he kept his eyes on his plate. Kyle said nothing, waiting for her to sit down, before beginning his meal. He ate quietly, steadily, rarely speaking. Once or twice he glanced up at Jenny. Meeting her eye, he looked away. A swelling giddiness was rising in her; she wanted to laugh at the two of them, but had the sense not to.

Clearing the dishes away at the end, she reached across him to pick up his glass, knowing the opened shirt revealed the dark shadow between her breasts.

His fist crashing down on the table startled her. She stood up and looked at him surprise.

'What the hell are you playing at now, Jenny?' His look raked over her. 'Since when have you become a damn tease?'

'Don't swear,' she said, looking down at the dish in her hand. Was that how it looked to him? She was suddenly embarrassed, ashamed.

'I'll talk however I want, dammit!' Kyle rose, towering over her. Reaching out, he wrenched the dishes from her hand, flinging them on the table. Taking her wrist in a none-too-gentle grasp, he pulled her from the room.

'Let me go. Don't!' Jenny protested as she was dragged down the hall, and then up the stairs. Fear began to make itself felt. 'Kyle, I'm sorry. Let me go.'

HARLEQUIN® DELIVERS FIRST-CLASS ROMANCE— DIRECT TO YOUR DOOR

Mail the Heart sticker on the postpaid order card today and you'll receive:

—4 new Harlequin Romance novels—FREE
—a beautiful manicure set—FREE
—and a surprise mystery bonus—FREE

But that's not all. You'll also get:

Money-Saving Home Delivery

When you subscribe to Harlequin Romance, the excitement, romance and faraway adventures of these novels can be yours for previewing in the convenience of your own home at less than retail prices. Every month we'll deliver 8 new books right to your door. If you decide to keep them, they'll be yours for only $1.99 each. That's 26¢ less per book than you would pay in a store—plus 89¢ for postage and handling per shipment.

Special Extras—FREE

Because our home subscribers are our most valued readers, we'll be sending you additional free gifts from time to time as a token of our appreciation.

OPEN YOUR MAILBOX TO A WORLD OF LOVE AND ROMANCE EACH MONTH. JUST COMPLETE, DETACH AND MAIL YOUR FREE OFFER CARD TODAY!

You'll love your beautiful manicure set—
an elegant and useful accessory, compact
enough to carry in your handbag. Its rich
burgundy case is a perfect expression of
your style and good taste—and it's yours
free with this offer!

Harlequin Romance™

FREE OFFER CARD

4 FREE BOOKS

**FREE MANICURE
SET**

**FREE MYSTERY
BONUS**

PLACE
HEART
STICKER
HERE

**MONEY-SAVING
HOME DELIVERY**

**MORE SURPRISES
THROUGHOUT THE
YEAR—FREE**

☑ **YES!** Please send me four Harlequin Romance
novels, *free*, along with my free manicure set and
my free mystery gift, as explained on the opposite page.

318 CIH WAUR

NAME _____

ADDRESS_____ APT. _____

CITY _____ PROVINCE _____

POSTAL CODE _____

Terms and prices subject to change.
Offer limited to one per household and
not valid to present subscribers.

PRINTED IN U.S.A.

Remember! To receive your free books, manicure set and mystery gift, return the postpaid card below. But don't delay!

DETACH AND MAIL CARD TODAY.

Business Reply Mail

No Postage Stamp Necessary if Mailed in Canada

Postage will be paid by

Harlequin Reader Service®
P.O. Box 609
Fort Erie, Ontario
L2A 9Z9

Canada Post Postes Canada
125

MAIL THE POSTPAID CARD TODAY!

'Like hell, I will,' he growled out. Kicking open his door, he dragged Jenny into his room and slammed the door behind them.

'Kyle——' she began, but was stopped when he went to sit on the bed and pulled her down on top of him, his mouth shutting hers, stopping all protest.

This was what she wanted, wasn't it? Her senses were clamouring for more as his hands were hard against her, holding her to him on the bed, drawing her very soul with his kiss.

When he rolled her over on her back, Jenny felt as if she had been jolted with volts of electricity. She grew hot as his mouth moved against hers, as his hard hands gentled a little, slipping to the buttons of her blouse and finishing the unfastening she had begun.

The touch of his warm fingers on her soft skin trailed fire on her already overheated body. She could feel her breasts fill with desire, harden to his touch, her nipples thrusting against the lacy bra. With a quick movement, he had unfastened that article of clothing, drawing it from her, freeing her to his gaze, to his touch.

His eyes darkened to black velvet as he looked at her, raising his eyes to her gaze, his hand cupping her breasts, gently caressing their fullness.

'You're as pretty as I thought you'd be,' he said in a throaty growl.

She smiled shyly, pleased beyond everything that he thought so, that he had said so.

Desire rose in Jenny, but she wanted him to know, 'Kyle, I wasn't being a tease.'

'Last night no, tonight yes?' he said, as her fingers unbuttoned his shirt, spreading the material so his chest could lie against hers.

She nodded, emotions so full she could barely breath. 'Kiss me. Please,' she whispered.

His eyes flared before he covered her mouth with his, his chest warm and hard against hers, his fingers trailing flames of desire and longing along her skin, her ribs, to her stomach.

The distant sound of the telephone gradually penetrated.

'Let it ring,' Kyle said against her throat, his hot lips moving against her skin, moving now to her ear, gently nibbling the lobe, his tongue teasing, tasting, moving on.

'That reminds me,' Jenny said guiltily. 'Jason Sperry called earlier, he has some information you want. He said to call him back.'

Kyle went still, then slowly sat up.

'Blast, that might be him now. I'd better get it.'

With a regretful look at Jenny, he swiftly rose and crossed the room, flinging open the door.

Jenny could hear him running down the stairs, and answering the phone.

As the soft drone of his conversation continued, she surmised it was Jason calling again. She should have told Kyle when he first came in. Then they would not have been interrupted.

She drew her shirt across her. She was cool without Kyle's hot body to warm her. As she lay there her eyes drifted around the room. It was twilight, soon to be night. She could make out the dresser, the open wardrobe door, revealing his clothes. The lamp by the bed, his travel clock. Then her eyes found the photograph.

Trying to focus on it, Jenny raised up on her arm, reaching for it. She switched on the lamp to see better, and her heart sank as she saw the lovely blonde girl, dressed in jeans and a casual blue shirt, smiling gaily back at her.

Scribbled across the bottom of the photograph were the words *For Kyle, Love Always, Cindy.*

Jenny stared at the face: alive, vibrant, her smile so radiant. Who was Cindy? Why was her picture on Kyle's dresser? Why indeed, unless she was his girl. Or his wife.

For a long time, Jenny looked at Cindy, almost unaware of the thoughts churning in her head. What, after all, did she know about Kyle Martin? She only knew the little he'd told her, and if he were making up things for the citizens of Palmer, why not be making up things to tell her as well?

Like what? she thought. He'd told her nothing. Was he married? Out for a fling? Or was he single and the devoted only son of a widowed mother?

She carefully replaced the picture, rose and quickly left the room without a backward glance. She couldn't stay. The picture only showed her how little she knew about the man. While her senses longed for his touch, her mind knew she needed more before giving herself to any man.

It was late when Kyle finally came back up. Jenny feigned sleep when he opened her door and looked into her room. He left and she let the tears slowly fall.

CHAPTER SEVEN

ON Saturday, Jenny stayed as far away from Kyle as she could. She didn't want to face him. She rose early, grabbed a quick breakfast, and took Shasta into town. She delivered all the accounts she had worked on during the week, got her mail from the post office box and went shopping for a new dress for George Carlisle's barbecue that night.

She refused to examine the reason why she wanted a new dress. George would be putting on a nice spread, and she wanted to look her best. It was really her first party since Johnny's death.

She thought of Johnny for a moment, missing him, wishing things were the way they had been a couple of years ago. She found she couldn't concentrate, however. With a rueful sigh, she acknowledged that Johnny was in the past, her past, gone for ever. No matter how much she wished it different, it was as it was. And she must let it go.

Kyle's dark eyes swam before her, his sardonic grin, his tall frame. She shook her head to dispel the image. Why was she always thinking about him? It would have to change. She paused on the pavement, briefly fantasising that she knew him better, that theirs was a normal friendship, growing in love. Would they marry? Was her mother right in that she should remarry?

She shook her head. Admonishing Shasta to wait for her, she went into the store in search of the perfect dress.

She arrived home just in time to go up and get ready for the barbecue. She showered, dried her hair and donned her new dress, pleased with her choice. It was a short batiste cotton in blue, which brought out the colour in her eyes. Fitted in the bodice, it swirled softly against her legs as she walked. Putting on high-heeled sandals, she was ready. Informally dressed, yet appropriate for the coming event.

Kyle was waiting in the living-room when she walked down. He rose when she came into view and Jenny was instantly conscious of him with every inch of her body. Would she always feel so breathless, almost faint, when around him? And how much longer would he be around?

He wore designer jeans, snug and low on his hips. Polished boots shod his feet and a dark brown, cotton-knit turtle-neck shirt covered his chest. She thought the clothes unseemly, a momentary flare of jealousy that every woman there would notice him. His shoulder muscles were outlined and enhanced with the chocolate shirt, his jeans almost too snug as her eyes were drawn to them.

'Too tight?' Kyle mocked, a devilish glint in his eye. Had he read her mind?

Jenny flushed, raising her eyes to meet the amusement in his. She could feel the heat in her face. It wasn't fair. He seemed to know exactly what she was thinking.

'Not if you don't think so. Can you walk?'

His laughter surprised her, forced an answering smile from her.

'As long as you don't get too close to me,' he replied audaciously.

'We'd better go,' she said, ignoring his laughter.

Jenny drove, concentrating on the road, trying vainly to ignore the man next to her. They were not the first to arrive, but the line of cars behind them on the driveway assured them they were not late. Jenny recognised most of the guests on the lawn, and the ones still arriving. It seemed as if George had invited most of the town.

'Jenny! Welcome.' George greeted them, leaning over to give her a kiss on the cheek.

'Hi, George. It's a nice turn out, and the weather's great.'

'It will be a mild night. Kyle, glad you could come.' George shook hands and glanced around. 'You know people, Jenny, introduce Kyle. As soon as all the guests have arrived, I'll have some time to spend with you. Save supper for me.'

Jenny was a trifle surprised by the request, but smiled. 'See you later,' she replied non-committally.

Kyle moved close to Jenny, taking her soft upper arm in his fingers. She instinctively pressed his hand against her side.

'Not now, sweetheart,' he said, rubbing his fingers against the side of her breast. 'Why did you leave last night?'

Jenny caught her breath, her knees going weak. 'I . . . I didn't know how long you'd be . . .' she lied. His fingers rubbed gently as he surveyed the crowd. Jenny wished they hadn't come, that they had stayed home and . . .

'I want you to tell me who everyone is. Point out the ones we've talked about. I'll let you know who I want to meet,' Kyle said, business back in hand.

Jenny blinked. Of course, Kyle was on a job. It was not a social outing for him. For a brief moment, she'd forgotten.

They wandered to the bar, Jenny greeting friends and acquaintances, giving names and thumbnail sketches on each of the various people to Kyle as they strolled along and he was introduced. Kyle had the background on almost everyone in attendance, but matching up faces with names took a little while.

'Nate Wilson.' Jenny nodded to a dark man across the patio who raised his glass to her. She smiled saucily and turned to Kyle. 'You two almost met last February, remember?'

He glanced at Wilson, back at Jenny. 'I remember. What does he do again?'

'Nate works at the garage in town.'

'Right. Who's the girl talking to him?'

Jenny hadn't seen Kyle glance at Nate again. Yet, sure enough, there was a tall blonde laughing at something Nate said, moving closer to him to hear better. Did Kyle go for tall blondes? Was the girl in the picture tall? Jenny was suddenly tired, drained.

'It's Naomi Taylor. Her father works at the mill, in the office. Naomi works in San Francisco. She must be on vacation or just up for the weekend.'

They were on their second drink when George joined them, smoothly drawing Jenny along with him. In only a short time he and Jenny were part of a large group of friends, laughing and joking. Of Kyle she lost track.

Susie Lewis joined them, pulling Jenny aside for a few moments of town gossip.

Once or twice as the evening progressed, Jenny saw Kyle. Sometimes talking with one group or another, once standing alone on the sidelines, watching what was going on around him.

Peggy and Dan O'Neil arrived, greeted their daughter and were soon drawn in to the circle of neighbours discussing the events of the summer yet to come: the Fourth of July fireworks display, the upcoming county fair.

'Great party, don't you think, Jenny?' Susie asked, as the daylight faded. Patio lamps came on, giving soft illumination to the scene.

Jenny pinned a bright smile on her face. Only moments before her parents had arrived, she had seen Kyle and Naomi slipping away from their group. Jenny refused to admit the party had lost its sparkle for her.

'Sure is. What's the latest on your Hawaiian vacation?'

The topic brought forth a long narrative on Susie's part of the plans she had made for the long dreamed of vacation she was taking in August.

As the night grew darker, the party bloomed. There was music for those who wanted to dance on the patio, a pool for those who had thought to bring a swimsuit. The food and drinks flowed steadily. Jenny felt her head begin to whirl.

She moved to one of the wooden benches near the house, getting a Coke in passing.

'Sitting this one out?' George joined her on the bench, nodding to the gyrating crowd on the patio.

'For a while. I've had my last drink for tonight. Coke for me from now on.' She raised her glass. 'It's a great party, George, thanks for having me. I'm having fun.'

'The way you say it almost makes you sound surprised. We're all your friends, Jenny.'

'I know. I'd almost forgotten. I need to get out more.'

George reached out and took her hand, gently holding it in his. 'I'd like to be a part of your getting out more.'

She smiled and nodded, looking at her Coke. That would be fine. George was easy to be with, not like some men she knew! He was safe, steady and reliable.

When George leaned over to kiss her, Jenny looked up in surprise, first at George, then over his shoulder, and her glance clashed with Kyle's. His look burned, but before Jenny could do anything, he turned and was lost from view.

'Couldn't resist,' George said, smiling. 'Come on, a slow song is starting and we can dance.'

Jenny danced for the next few hours: with George, with her Dad, with friends of Johnny, of her folks, of George. She looked for Kyle, found him once or twice dancing with Naomi. Always with Naomi. A twist of jealousy penetrated. She tossed her hair and threw herself into enjoyment of the dance, yet it persisted.

Finally, Jenny had had enough. She would find Kyle and tell him she was ready to go home. It was late and she was tired; they still had a long ride home and she wanted to leave before she got too sleepy to drive.

She scanned the patio, but there was no sign of him. Going through the house, she searched for him in vain. Where could he be? She went to the truck, but still there was no sign of him. Jenny was torn between being worried about the man, and annoyed he was so elusive.

Walking slowly back to the patio again she heard a soft giggle to her right. Glancing towards the edge of the house, she could see a couple locked in an embrace. The light spilling from the house cast them in a soft glow, the blonde hair of the girl in sharp contrast to the dark hair of the man holding her.

Jenny stopped, rooted to the spot. So much for wanting to sleep with her, he was out for whatever he could get. Jenny felt the heat rise in her cheeks. God, she was glad nothing had happened between them!

Nothing? her mind queried.

'Kyle?'

The couple looked up, and stepped apart.

'I'm tired and want to go home. Are you almost ready, or do you want to get a ride from someone else?' Jenny kept her tone even, kept her eyes on his outline, ignoring Naomi.

'Give me a few minutes.'

'I'll wait in the truck.'

She turned and blindly stumbled her way to the truck. She climbed in and leaned her head back against the seat. She refused to think. The ache she was feeling in her chest was probably just indigestion. Every time an image danced before her eyes, she blanked it out. She would *not* think.

The sudden glare of light when Kyle opened the door made her blink. She sat up and inserted the key into the ignition.

'Jenny——' he started.

'Not tonight, Kyle. I'm too tired.'

'Want me to drive?'

She hesitated, then nodded.

He slammed his door closed and walked around, his feet crunching on the gravel. She slid over on the seat and looked out the window of the passenger door as he climbed in. She rested her head against the back of the seat, tired, drained. She was not used to such late nights, to excessive drinking, and the dancing. Not used to daydreams of delights to come and the cruel shock of reality. She was so tired.

He must have a good sense of direction, she thought drowsily as they drove quickly over the distance to her home. He never asked directions, she never volunteered any, yet in only a short time they were home.

'Jenny——' he began, as he shut off the engine.

A flare of anger sparked in her.

'No! I don't want to hear some made-up story,' she stormed back. 'What do you do, lust after anything in a skirt? Me one night, Naomi the next?'

'No.' His voice was hard in the dark. 'You're a fine one to talk! What about George's kisses?'

'George is a friend, someone I've known for years. And it was only a light kiss!'

'Naomi is business.'

'And what am I? Perks, that's what you said. How do you keep it all straight?'

'I have no trouble keeping it straight.'

He reached out and took the back of her head in his hand, bringing her up to him, ready for his kiss. Jenny held herself stiffly but was lost when his lips touched hers. She swayed towards him, angry he could make her feel like this, angry she wouldn't, couldn't pull back. The touch of him, his mouth against hers, his fingers tangled in her hair, the press of his shoulder, was intoxicating. On top of all she had had to drink, Jenny wasn't sure if she could stand it. Her thoughts were spinning, or was it her head? Time stood still.

When he released her to take a deep breath, she pulled back, glaring at him in the dark, sorry she couldn't see him, sorry he couldn't see how angry she was at him—or was it at herself for responding?

'Anyone handy will do, right?' she snapped to his silhouette.

'Jenny...'

'No, just leave me alone!' She threw open her door and stumbled out beside the truck. Slamming the door hard enough to rock the truck, she started towards the house, her head still spinning. She tripped and Kyle was there.

'You drive me crazy,' she muttered. 'I don't think I can even make it inside. My head is spinning.'

He chuckled. 'Come on, baby, I'll carry you.'

'No, you can't...'

Before she could react, Kyle scooped her up, his left arm beneath her shoulders.

'You have to help, my arm can't take your full weight.'

Jenny put her arms around his neck, to help take her weight from his arm. Her cheek pressed against

Kyle and she closed her eyes as he took her inside and up the stairs. Her head was whirling.

'I'm so tired,' she whispered as he put her on her bed.

'I know.'

'You should have stayed with Naomi,' she murmured, burrowing down in her pillow. In only a minute she'd be asleep and could forget all this.

'I don't want Naomi, I want you.' He kissed her mouth and left.

Jenny smiled and drifted to sleep.

'Tell me about the relationship between Nate Wilson and George Carlisle.' Kyle came into the kitchen the next morning as Jenny was making coffee.

'Huh? Good morning. Nate and George?'

'Yes.'

Kyle was dressed in black cords, boots and a dark, checked shirt. His manner was businesslike, his face tight, closed. Last night was over, it was back to business.

'Well, what exactly do you want to know? They're neighbours, sort of. They've known each other for years, but Nate is really Nick's friend. He and Nick and Johnny were kids together, older than I, younger than George. If he and George are friends I'd be surprised, but only because of the age difference and the difference in what they do.'

'And what do you know about Nate?'

'He runs the garage for old Mr Benson. He was born here, his folks live near Strawberry. He's never been in trouble with the law, if that's what you want to know. Why? Do you suspect Nate's involved in this? Is that why he was after you last winter?'

Kyle was silent for a moment. 'And Naomi?'

Jenny flashed a grimace and shrugged. 'I don't know. Friends with Nate, I guess, because they were in the same grade in school. Maybe George takes her out. Why don't you ask her?'

'I'm asking you.'

'I don't know.'

'She smokes pot, you know.'

'No!' Jenny swung around to face him. 'I didn't know, how do you?'

'She was smoking it last night. I was watching her.'

'Where did she get it? From here? Or San Francisco?'

'That's what I'm going to find out.'

Jenny put his coffee before him. 'How?'

'Chat up Naomi. Got her phone number?'

Jenny felt sick. 'It's in the book, under Charles Taylor. Look it up.' She sipped her coffee.

Kyle's fingers beneath her chin were cool as he raised her face to his.

'Don't get into a temper, pet. I told you last night she's work, you're not.'

'Perk?'

'Right.' He leaned over and kissed her, his tongue teasing hers. 'Ummm, you taste good. Can I use the truck today?'

'Sure, by all means, let me do all I can to further that relationship!' Her sarcasm was lost when all he said was, 'Thanks.'

Jenny cleaned up from breakfast, with the low murmur of Kyle's voice in the background as he talked to Naomi Taylor. Deciding to take Shasta for a long hike, and a picnic, Jenny prepared a lunch for them.

She wanted to get out of the house, away from things that reminded her of Kyle, with his charming, sexy manner one minute, his all-business approach the next. What she did *not* want to do was think of him with Naomi. She didn't want to envisage them talking, exchanging information, growing closer.

She wanted to know more about Kyle herself, to learn where he grew up, what had decided him on his career, why he was here. How was she to know, however, if any answers to her questions would be truthful? If he wanted more cover, he'd tell her whatever he wanted.

Jenny went to get her backpack and change into her hiking boots. She would get away and think of nothing, just enjoy the pleasant afternoon with Shasta. She'd done just fine with her life before the advent of Mr Kyle Martin. Chin firmly in the air, she marched down the hall.

Kyle reached out his hand as she passed, clasping her fingers in his, pulling her to a stop beside him.

'I'll be there around noon, then.' He hung up and swung her hand loosely back and forth.

'What are you going to do today?'

Trying to tug her hand free, to no avail, Jenny frowned. 'What do you care? You've made your plans.'

'Come on, Jen, I told you it was work. What are you going to do?'

'Take a hike.'

'Jenny,' he said warningly, drawing himself up to his full height, his eyes narrowed as he towered over her.

'I'm going to take Shasta and go for a hike,' she enunciated very clearly and distinctly, eyes sparkling.

'Where?'

Yanking her hand free, she rubbed her fingers, though they really didn't need it. 'Just in the hills. How far can I get?' She was scathing. 'You'll have my truck.'

'I don't know when I'll be home.' Kyle watched her through narrowed eyes.

She swallowed as she looked at him—so tall, dark, masculine. His shoulders were broad, tapering to narrow hips. He wore his jeans low, tight. Jenny's eyes guiltily rose to his face again, to meet the slight amusement in his eyes. Was it her fault her eyes were drawn to his tight jeans? If he wanted to flaunt it . . .

Naomi would get the full effect. *She* was business. Jenny was only a perk. Well, Kyle could just find himself another perk! She did not relish the thought of providing a light dalliance for Kyle as he worked, only to be cast aside and forgotten when the assignment was over.

She pulled away, turned and continued upstairs, leaning over the railing to call softly, 'Have fun today. . . I will!'

Kyle was in the den when she left. She paused near the door, then went on through to the kitchen, calling Shasta to join her. She knew that when she returned, Kyle would be gone. To be with Naomi.

Working, he *said*. She grabbed her knapsack and left. She didn't want to think of *that* work.

The day was warm and pleasant as they started off, going towards the west, towards an area of the mountains Jenny rarely explored. There was a rough spot of scrub and rocks before beckoning meadows beyond. Usually she didn't care to try to traverse the awkward portion, but today she wanted the challenge, wanted something to keep her mind off Kyle Martin and his disturbing presence.

The backpack was heavy with her food and soda, and the small portion of meat she had brought for Shasta. The homeward journey would be easier, with most of the weight gone.

Jenny tried to keep her thoughts from Kyle as she scrambled across the hillside, moved down to sparsely forested land. The dapple shade from the ponderosa pines and Douglas fir provided a welcome relief from the heat as the day grew warmer. Jeans and hiking boots were warm, but she knew better than to try to hike in shorts. Scratches from branches, and scrapes from rocks when she fell, would be her due if she didn't have the protective covering. But it was hot.

They had come a long way. Shasta no longer ran ahead, but trotted by Jenny's side. Alert, ears constantly twitching, but no longer fresh. Jenny was growing tired, too. The next likely spot and they'd stop; eat and rest, maybe take a small nap. Jenny smiled at the thought. It would be a pleasant way to while away the hours.

Breaking out of a group of trees, she found the sheltered meadow. It was large, hidden away from the beaten track, surrounded by soaring pines and firs.

Jenny paused at its edge and looked across the expanse, a frown growing as she saw the plant flourishing across the gentle slope. Slowly she walked to the green growth, staring at it, reaching out to touch, to pluck a small leaf.

Stuart Brownley had shown her marijuana in its various stages, at their museum. This was stage number one. The young, growing plant.

Jenny sank down, amazed at the crop spread before her. There had to be over an acre of the stuff. Every cleared inch of the meadow was planted with it.

A faint unease, a growing dread and fear began to course up her back. Hastily she glanced around, afraid of unseen eyes, afraid of who might be guarding this field.

She rose and snapped her fingers for Shasta, moving steadily back into the forest, up the hillside, looking for a sheltered spot, a safe place.

Seeing a boulder with an overhang, she crawled up to it, sank in its shadow and scanned the hillside. Nothing moved.

Jenny carefully put the little leaf down, opened her backpack and shared lunch with Shasta. The big Shepherd dog ate his meat, then sank his head on his paws, watching as Jenny ate her lunch, slowly munching and constantly searching the hillside.

She was finished and ready to move, to get back home and tell Kyle what she'd found, when Shasta raised his head and began growling. The fur on the back of his neck stood up, his ears were perked forward, his lips drawn back, as the low growl continued.

Jenny swallowed, eyes straining to see what the dog had seen, to know what danger lurked. She saw nothing, yet Shasta had his eyes fixed on a spot part way down the hill, near the trees. The throaty growl changed to a hoarse bark as he stood, eyes riveted on the trees.

Jenny shrank back against the boulder. Who was there? What was there?

Suddenly a deer bounded from cover, scampering across the open space, Shasta in hot pursuit.

'Shasta!' Jenny called, standing, relief almost overwhelming her. 'Shasta, come!'

The dog stopped, barked twice more at the vanishing deer and turned to trot meekly back to his mistress.

'You scared me to death,' she scolded, gathering up the wilted marijuana leaf, wrapping it carefully in a napkin and putting it into her knapsack. Slinging it on her shoulders, she started off. Carefully committing the landmarks to memory, Jenny walked cautiously back the way she'd come. She wanted to be sure she could bring Kyle back here, could find her way again. He'd want to see for himself.

It was late when she reached home. But Kyle was still gone. She had forgotten his *work* with Naomi. Fretting as the minutes dragged by, Jenny constantly watched the drive for his return, anxious to tell him all she had learned.

Night fell, still he hadn't returned. Jenny ate a light supper, growing more and more frustrated with Kyle's absence. Darn the man, how much time did he have to spend with Naomi? Just what kind of work was it, anyway?

Jenny woke the next morning, a strange ache in her breast. She had stayed up until after midnight, waiting for Kyle's return. He had not come by the time she went to sleep. She lay in bed, trying to hear if he were here now or not, afraid to find he was not.

She got up, dressed and went down to get breakfast. The door to Kyle's room was still open. She peeped in—the bed still made. He had not come last night! He had stayed with Naomi.

CHAPTER EIGHT

JENNY was lying in the sun in the yard when she heard the sound of the truck. Her eyes clenched tightly closed, and her breathing became constricted. She would not greet him ... blast the man! She had been excited by her discovery yesterday, anxious to tell him about it, show him the field. As the night passed, her disappointment had built into anger. Let him find it himself. If he wouldn't share his clues with her, why should she with him?

She had left the wilted marijuana leaf at his place in the kitchen. If he wanted to see more, he could find it himself, or maybe Naomi could show him the way!

The sound of his steps on the gravel, then on the grass alerted her to his arrival. He must have spotted her as he drove in.

'Hi.'

She opened one eye, closed it again.

There was a sigh, then he sat down on the grass beside her.

'Had breakfast already?' he asked.

'Yes, hours ago. Didn't Naomi feed you?'

'I wasn't with Naomi.'

Jenny thought she heard surprise in his tone. If not with Naomi, where had he been all night?

His fingers encircled her arms, pulling her upright, close to his face. Jenny's eyes opened in surprise, her breathing erratic. His brown eyes held a

117

trace of amusement as he stared down into her startled blue ones, then dropped to her mouth. Jenny licked suddenly dry lips.

'I ran out of gas.'

She started to scoff, then stopped, closing her eyes in sudden confusion. 'Oh, I forgot to tell you, the gas gauge is broken.' She opened her eyes warily.

'I found out. A mile out of town, about midnight! I hiked back to town for gas, only to find the station closes at eleven.'

Jenny was conscious of his hands, warm on her arms, his breath fanning her face as he talked to her, his voice remaining even. It was hard to concentrate on what he was saying.

'So what did you do?'

'Went to sleep at your folks'!'

'What?' Jenny sat up, pulled away and stared at him. 'You're kidding!'

'Nope. You dad's a nice man. Not easily flustered. It must have been a bit much having a stranger wake you up at midnight and ask for a bed! Fortunately for me your mother came down and issued the invitation. I got to sleep in your old room.'

Jenny grinned, then laughed at the picture he painted. 'I would have thought a big, brave government agent would have dossed down at the side of the road,' she scoffed.

'Not convalescent ones,' he said lazily. 'Otherwise, of course, I would have pushed that big truck of yours back to the gas station, ripped off the lock with my bare teeth and filled the tank.'

She giggled at that. 'Sure,' she jeered.

'Doubt me, eh?' Kyle reached for her again, pushing her against the blanket she had been lying on, coming down to cover her chest with his, pinning her hands over her head as his mouth sought, and found hers.

Jenny gave a sigh of pure delight as her tongue met his, teased it, invading his mouth. His fingers threaded through hers, tightened as he moved his lips, causing Jenny to lose track of time and thought. She could only feel the heavenly weight of him across her, the pleasure his mouth brought, the thrill of his touch as he moved to her cheeks, her neck, her throat. Vainly she struggled to bring down her hands as his mouth moved lower, his chin moving the cloth from his path, his hands pinioning hers firmly out of reach.

The warmth from his lips, his tongue on her soft breast forced a small moan from Jenny's mouth, spread the heat through her thighs, her stomach. Slowly she arched, moving to get more of her body beneath his, seeking what Kyle had wanted all along.

A cold, wet nose thrust its way between them.

'Shasta, get away!' Jenny shrieked, turning her head away from his tongue as he swiped the side of her face, then began barking at this new game.

'Damn it!' Kyle rolled away, trying to fend off the dog as Shasta continued to nose his way in, joining in on the fun.

Jenny scrambled to her knees, laughing at Kyle's efforts now, at Shasta's prancing and barking. It was all a game to him.

'Come on, big, brave drug agent, I'll get you some breakfast.'

Kyle got reluctantly to his feet, coming up to take her in his arms. Pulling her roughly against him, he leaned down to kiss her.

'We could continue upstairs, with the door shut on your friend,' he murmured after a long minute.

Jenny leaned against his hard, warm body, imprinting the feel of him on her mind. She wanted to hold on to this moment, for a few seconds pretend that that was what they'd do. But not for her the perks...

She drew back slowly, shook her head reluctantly. Her anger gone, she gave a tentative smile.

'No, come on and see what I found. You'll be surprised.'

And he was. Once he recognised it, he was all business: questioning Jenny as to where she had found it, how, and if any signs of who the field belonged to were in evidence.

'I can show you where it is. We can explore it in detail.'

'No! Just tell me. I'll do the exploring.'

'I want to go,' she said stubbornly.

'No! Just tell me where it is.'

'Well, I won't. If you don't let me go, you can look for it yourself.' She waved her arm around her. 'You have the whole Sierra Nevada to look, so get to it.' She stormed out of the kitchen.

'Jenny!' Kyle went right after her, stopping her in the hall, swinging her around to face him, his hands gripping her upper arms tightly. 'This is no game. The men involved in this are dangerous. They could be killers. I don't want you involved.'

'I am involved. I'm providing cover for you. What do you think will happen if you go traipsing off by yourself? If we go together, we can...can picnic. Be having an innocent outing, if anyone should ask. I think it's safer that way.'

Besides, I don't want you to go alone. She knew it was dangerous and she didn't want Kyle to have to face it alone, not now. Not until he was fit and could cope. She knew he had a job to do, and was probably used to going into danger. But it was different when he was fit. He was still convalescing, whether or not he'd admit it. She didn't want him to go alone.

He looked down into her face, indecision in his eyes. Jenny felt it was a new experience for him. Finally his fingers slackened a little.

'All right, just today. We'll go on a picnic. You pack a lunch. Make it big, I'm hungry.'

Jenny led the way, backpack on her shoulders. Kyle had argued for it, but she had insisted, it was hers and her size. In reality she was sparing his shoulder, but knew he was too much of a man to let her have it for that reason. He had showered and changed before they started out, tight jeans covered by a loose-fitting shirt. Jenny eyed his outfit for a moment.

'Carrying a gun?' she asked softly.

'Yes,' was the bit out reply.

She recognised the landmarks she had so carefully committed to memory. The way was still hard, and seemed longer today.

'You hike a lot, don't you?' Kyle said, moving to walk beside her.

'Yes, I love to be out in the open, to see all the empty land, the beauties of the mountains.'

'It reminds me a little of picnics my family went on when I was a kid,' he murmured. 'We didn't live in the mountains, though. San Diego was home, but the long endless beaches and vast ocean give one the same sort of peace.'

'Are you an only child?' Jenny could scarcely believe he was opening up. She knew this was not part of a cover story. Kyle was sharing a portion of his life with her.

'I had a sister. She and my folks and I used to go to the beach a lot when I was young. It all changed, once I went to college.'

'Where did you go?'

'Berkeley. How about you? I know you grew up here, but have you ever gone anywhere else?'

'Sure, lots of places. I went to college in Sacramento, to Disneyland one summer, the Grand Canyon and skiing in the Rockies. I have all I want here.' She smiled at him. 'I know it doesn't seem likely to you, but I found Sacramento a big city. I was amazed at Los Angeles and San Francisco. I prefer the mountains.'

'I can see why. I've been all over the state, back East too, and this area is one of the prettiest I've seen.'

Shasta ran alongside them, sometimes surging ahead, sometimes lingering behind. Jenny instinctively slowed as they approached the meadow.

'Just ahead,' she said softly.

They stopped at the edge.

Kyle stood in silence for a long moment, assessing what was before them.

'Is it marijuana?' Jenny asked.

'Yes.' He shook his head slightly. 'Must have a street value of over half a million,' he said softly to himself.

'That much?' Jenny was surprised. There was a lot there, but that much? 'It doesn't look like such a big crop.'

'Who owns this land?'

'I'm not sure, but I think it's national forest land. That stream we crossed a while back runs along the boundary on this side. We can check it on the map when we get back.'

'Stay here, and hold Shasta. I'm going to circle the field. Wait for me here, understand?' His eyes were hard, narrowed against the sun, as he looked at Jenny.

She nodded and sank down on the soft pine needles, holding Shasta's collar. She watched as Kyle slowly started down the hill, hugging the shelter of the trees, skirting the meadow, slowly working his way around. After a while she lost sight of him and sat idly watching the field, the butterflies dancing across the lacy plants, the hot sun burning in the sky, the soft pattern of the pine and fir limbs throwing shade where she was sitting. A slow depression settled on Jenny as she sat and watched the plants move in the slight breeze.

Kyle came up on her left side and dropped down beside her. She glanced at him questioningly, but he shook his head.

'There's a road near the end of the field, about fifty yards off. That's probably how they plan to harvest it. They've got an elaborate irrigation set up, they must pipe water in from the river occasionally. The sun's too hot to grow the plant without some irrigation. I wonder how often they water.' He was silent for a long moment, assessing the field. 'Who it is, though, is anyone's guess.' He looked at her, and sensed her mood.

'What's wrong?'

'All this.' She waved her hand towards the meadow. 'I never believed it, you know. Brownley was like something out of James Bond. I would be doing a service to my country. Then you came, and sometimes I believed it, but mostly you were just like anyone else. It was like playing a game. But now I do believe it. Someone in Palmer is tied up in this. I just wish it had never happened here. That it had happened somewhere else and left my part of the world clean.'

'Everyone everywhere wishes that. Have you ever tried it?' Kyle asked.

'No. Have you?'

'Yes, once or twice in college. Experiments. I was brash, a know-it-all, then.'

Jenny glanced at him with a small, tight smile; she didn't see any change since then.

'I didn't like it, and quit. I don't like to feel out of control.'

'No, you like to be in control.'

'All the time,' he agreed.

Jenny nodded, she couldn't imagine him any other way.

'Continued use causes problems. You can see lots of old winos, but you never see an old drug addict.' His voice grew bitter, his face closed.

'What will you do now?'

'Put in a stake-out when harvest time grows closer. See if we can find out who's behind this.'

'And Naomi?' Jenny couldn't resist asking.

Kyle slanted her a grin and rose, holding his hand to help her to her feet.

'Continue on that line, as well. That's the retail side, this is the wholesale side. Maybe the same group is running the whole damned show.'

Jenny wished she had not asked. She turned as they started up the hillside, drawing back farther into the woods, leaving the meadow behind them. When they reached a cleared, flat, rocky area, she turned to Kyle.

'Want to eat here?'

'Fine.'

They shared the sandwiches and sodas she had brought, lying back on a light blanket she had packed. Shasta gnawed on the bone Jenny had carried for him, content in the hot sun.

They talked desultorily about other times and friends. Jenny told Kyle about her life in Palmer, answering his questions when he raised them, questioning him in turn.

'And you never married?' she asked at last.

'Nope, too much going on. This life would be too much to ask of a wife. The uncertain hours, the long time away on assignments.'

'Not to mention the risks, the dangers,' she murmured.

He shrugged. 'And you? I hear Johnny's been dead over a year. Will you look to remarry one day?'

Jenny gazed over the rocky hillside to the distant blue haze over the ridges of the far ranges. 'I thought at one time never again; while being married is nice, the pain of losing is too great.'

'And now?'

'Who knows?' Who knows, she repeated in her head. If things had been different, if things were different, she might have loved Kyle Martin.

As the day grew warmer, and the talk died, Jenny shrugged out of her button-up shirt. She had a sun-top on, cotton, with spaghetti straps. She turned her face up to the sun, glad for its warmth, the peace in the clearing.

Kyle opened his shirt, laying back on his arms for a moment, then sitting up to rub his injured shoulder. Taking off his shirt, he used it as a pillow for his head, lying down in the sun.

Jenny looked at him. His chest was broad and muscular, his arms and shoulders showing a strength and fitness that had been hinted at beneath his shirts. The angry red gash high on his left arm showed where the bullet had penetrated; she winced, imagining the pain and anguish it had caused. There was one other scar on his body, faded now, obviously an old one, low on his chest. The gun protruded from the waistband of his jeans.

How could he constantly put himself in danger? Didn't he want to put that behind him and get a safe profession? She frowned at the thought of another incident that would injure him. How much longer could he do it? Did government agents work until they were sixty-five and retire? Would he move on to something else? What else, she wondered, could he do?

Her eyes moved up to his head, his brown hair ruffled and blown by the hike, his eyes slits, watching her look at him. She blushed in confusion, and

looked away, afraid the hunger she felt was reflected in her face.

'Want to make love here in the sun?' he asked
softly, his hand trailing fire down her arm, his warm
fingers closing over hers.

She looked around. They were alone, just the two
of them on a deserted hillside.

'What, you, me and Shasta?'

'Shasta has his bone, he won't bother us.'

Jenny licked her lips, her heart tripping in excitement, and anticipation. She turned to look at Kyle.
Shasta stopped gnawing and raised his head towards the woods, a low growl in his throat.

Kyle sat up, looking where the dog was.

'It's only a deer,' Jenny said in disgust. 'He did
that last time, too.'

Kyle turned and pushed her back on the blanket,
roughly putting his hand beneath her sun-top.

'Kyle, don't.' Jenny's hands ineffectively flut-
tered against his.

'Someone's coming, Jenny. Leave it.' He spread
her top and leaned against her, capturing her mouth
with his, moving his lips against her as she felt the
hard metal of the gun pushed beneath her bottom
with his other hand.

'Keep on this. Sit still, if it comes to it. If you're
forced to rise, try to drag the blanket over the gun.
Got it? Don't let anyone know we have it.'

Jenny nodded, the gun an uncomfortable bulge
beneath her. Her heart was tripping rapidly now,
but not in anticipation. She strained to hear what
Kyle had heard. Soon footsteps climbing the rocky
hillside were audible.

Kyle raised his head and glanced over his shoulder as if hearing the intruders for the first time. He glanced back at Jenny and winked.

'We've got company!'

He turned and sat up, drawing on his shirt, shielding her as the two men continued to climb towards them. Jenny recognised Nate Wilson, and Ben Waters, a man who worked at the mill.

She blushed and snatched her top closed, buttoning it and sitting up, conscious all the while of the gun hidden beneath her. She watched apprehensively as the men drew close and stopped.

'Hi, Jenny, Kyle.' Nate spoke first, a sly smile on his face.

Jenny blushed, looking at Kyle in confusion. What role was she to play?

'Hi, Nate, Ben.' Jenny nodded at the other man, bright colour high in her cheeks.

'On a picnic, I see,' Nate said, then scanned the area. 'I would have tried for a nice meadow, green grass.'

Kyle shrugged and looked around as well. 'We didn't see any on this hillside at all. Got hungry. Know of one?'

Nate looked at him for a moment, tense and poised, then shook his head. 'Nope. Some nice ones on the other side of Jenny's place, near the river. Not on this hillside.' His glance moved to Jenny, back to Kyle.

'It's a long trek back, let's get started, Kyle.' Jenny's low voice broke the tension. He looked at her and smiled.

'OK. I'll carry the knapsack. You carried it on the way here.'

She nodded and smiled shyly at Nate and Ben. They watched as Kyle gathered the remnants of lunch and stuffed it into the backpack.

Jenny pulled on her long-sleeved shirt, trying to button it with fingers that shook. She hoped the two men wouldn't notice. Why were they here? Were they involved with the marijuana? Or just out for a hike? She was suddenly glad they'd had the picnic. Even if Nate and Ben were involved in marijuana, they would not suspect Kyle of spying. They'd see it as an innocent outing. What if he had come alone?

Kyle took the corner of the blanket and pulled it up.

'I need to take the blanket, Jenny,' he said, his eyes trying to convey a message.

She nodded, wondering how to get up and not expose the gun.

'Shasta! Come on, boy,' she called as she rose to her knees. The two men swivelled to see the dog, then turned back to her. It was enough time. Kyle had the blanket bunched up and was stuffing it into the backpack.

'Come on, boy. Leave the bone. You can get another at home.' Jenny stood up and coaxed Shasta. He picked up the bone and pranced over to them.

'See you, Nate, Ben.' Jenny pasted a smile on her face and reached out her hand to Kyle. She was trembling, wanted to run away at full speed, but hoped it didn't show. He took her hand, squeezing it reassuringly when he felt her fingers tremble, the backpack slung over his right shoulder.

'Be seeing you,' Kyle said to the two silent men. They moved slowly away.

When they were out of hearing, Jenny said softly, out of the corner of her mouth, 'Are they still watching us? Do you think it's them?'

'I've no idea, but it raises interesting possibilities. And yes, I think they'll watch us off the mountain.'

He stopped and turned to her, pulling her into his arms and kissing her. With his eyes open, he glanced back to where they'd been. The two men were still watching.

'They're still there,' he said against her mouth. 'Let's go.'

The rest of the way home was silent. Jenny alternated between growing anger because Kyle had used her as subterfuge to cover why they were near the field, and wondering if Nate and Ben were really involved in drugs.

When they reached the house, Kyle handed her the backpack.

'I've got some calls to make. Be careful when you take out the gun.' He went into the den, pulling the hall phone into the room, and closed the door behind him.

Jenny stood staring after him. Who did he think he was? It was her house, her phone! He had just shut the door in her face! After a minute, she turned and stomped down the hall to the kitchen. Gingerly she unpacked the backpack and laid the gun at his place, facing towards the wall.

Jenny had taken her shower and was still brushing her hair in her room when she heard the shower running again. Kyle had obviously finished his phoning.

She went downstairs and sat on the front porch, gazing off into the hills while waiting for him to finish. She heard him coming down the stairs and looked over her shoulder into the house.

'I'm going out, Jenny. Can I borrow your truck again?'

'Sure. Where are you going?'

'I'll be back late. Don't wait up.' He turned and went back down the hall, evading the question, leaving before Jenny could catch up. She ran down the hall, but he was across the yard and into the pick-up, starting the engine.

'Blast you, Kyle Martin! If you're going to Naomi Taylor again, you can just stay there. Move out, like you wanted to,' she said, knowing he couldn't hear her. Knowing she really didn't mean it.

CHAPTER NINE

JENNY watched in frustration as the truck disappeared down the drive, then she turned slowly back to the house. Shasta followed her, bone in mouth.

'Not in the house, my boy. You eat that outside.' She held the door for him to go back outside. The phone rang and Jenny let the screen slam as she went to get it.

It was her mother.

'Did Kyle get home all right this morning? We tried calling earlier, but no one answered.'

'Yes, Mom, he did. We went for a picnic lunch, just got back a little while ago. Thanks for putting him up for the night.'

'You should have told him about the gauge.' Her mother's vague voice drifted across the wires, causing Jenny to smile.

'I know. Well, he knows now. How's Dad?'

'Fine. He'll say hello. George's party was fun, though a little wild, I thought.'

'Me, too, at the end.' Especially Kyle kissing Naomi! The thought caused Jenny to frown. She had forgotten that. What game was he playing? Saying he wanted her, yet when she said no, going off with the next available woman?

'Hello, sweetheart.' Her dad came on the line.

'Hi, Dad. Kyle told me about last night. Sorry he had to wake you up.'

'No problem. He's nice, though he doesn't look like Edith at all. You two come for dinner soon. We used to know Edith so well. I'm sorry we lost touch.'

'OK. I'll call later in the week and set something up.' If I can't get out of it first, Jenny thought. Just what they needed, someone who knew Edith well! And could soon find out Kyle didn't know her at all, much less was her son.

George Carlisle called later that evening.

'Thanks for having me to your barbecue,' Jenny said. 'It was my first big social outing since Johnny's death, and I'm glad it was at your place.'

'My pleasure. The only problem with being host is my time was spread so thin. I wanted to spend more time with you, Jenny. Would you be free for dinner this week? Tomorrow night, maybe?'

Jenny hesitated. She should be pleased someone asked her out, glad some male appeared to want to spend time in her company. Yet she was disappointed it wasn't Kyle.

Remembering his abrupt departure, she made up her mind.

'Yes, I could make it, thanks. I can be ready at six-thirty.'

'Good, see you then. We'll go into Tahoe, if you like.'

'That sounds like fun, I haven't been there in a while. Thanks for asking me, George.' That would show Mr Kyle Martin some people wanted to be with her!

Jenny watched TV that night, entertained by the movie, yet she kept one ear constantly attuned for the sound of the pick-up. Where was Kyle? What was he doing?

He had not returned by the time she went to bed. It was after midnight before the headlights swept across her wall, and the sound of the truck crunching the gravel was heard. She held her breath when he came in the house, tensed and straining to hear him. He climbed the stairs, seemed to pause near her door, then proceeded to his room. The door closed with a soft click and Jenny sighed, turning over to finally go to sleep.

Kyle was gone when she awoke the next morning. The pick-up was in the garage, and she used it to drive into town and get the next batch of work orders. It was a pleasant morning, warm and still. She was finished by noon and went to see if Susie was free for lunch.

Seated around the table at the small coffee shop, Susie was curious and talkative as Jenny smiled and tried to answer all her questions.

'Wasn't the party at George's super? I think most of the town was there. What did you think of Miss Naomi appropriating Johnny's cousin?' she asked unexpectedly.

Jenny blinked. So much for the possibility of Nate's spreading the tale of their picnic! If Susie didn't know, no one would.

'Well, Naomi is very attractive, and Kyle is used to the city. He teaches at San Francisco State.'

'Oh, so when he goes home, they might take right up.' Susie went off into a daydream, rhapsodising about a love affair that might originate right in their own home town.

Jenny didn't like the turn of the conversation. She was being silly, of course. Kyle wasn't really a professor at the State University, it was only his front, his cover. Still, the thought of his seeing Naomi rankled. She didn't want to think about it. It was work, he'd said, but what did that really mean? Moonlight and kisses to lull her into confiding in him? Surely government agents had other ways to question people.

Changing the subject, Jenny soon had Susie talking again about her upcoming vacation to Hawaii.

Kyle had not returned when Jenny went upstairs in the late afternoon to shower and get ready for dinner with George.

She felt vaguely guilty. She really didn't want to go out with George, she wasn't excited about going out at all. A quiet evening at home would suit her better. But George wasn't to know that. She had accepted his invitation and should make the most of it. It wasn't his fault she felt as she did.

She wore a soft rose silk dress and high heels, brushing her hair until the gold highlights showed in the late afternoon sun. A light application of make-up, a dab of *Joy* and she was ready. Taking a light shawl in case the evening turned cool, she left to wait for George downstairs.

'Going out?' Kyle's voice stopped her at the top of the steps. She turned; he was standing in the doorway to his room, clad only in his jeans. She hadn't heard his return.

She swallowed, nodded. 'Yes. George is taking me to dinner. I didn't fix you anything, I didn't know if you'd be home or not.'

'I can manage that. Where are you going?'

'I don't know. Lake Tahoe, I think.'

'That's a long drive.' Kyle moved to come up to Jenny, causing her to tilt her head back to see him. His eyes travelled over her body, coming back to rest on her eyes. Taking a deep breath, he smiled sardonically.

'The whole bit, eh?'

Jenny turned to go down the stairs, his hand shot out to grasp her arm and turn her back.

'Don't go, Jenny. Tell him you can't make it tonight. Some other time.' Kyle's voice was low, hurried.

'No, I won't. I can go out with whomever I wish. Please let me go.'

'I don't want you to go with George Carlisle.'

'Oh, come on, Kyle, you don't own me. I can see whomever I wish!'

'Not George.' He moved his hand to her shoulder, the thumb gently caressing her collarbone. Jenny felt her resolution dissolving. His hand burned through her silk dress, moving seductively against her. She swayed towards him and glanced at him through her lashes. The triumphant gleam in his eyes jerked her back.

'No! I won't be manipulated!' She shrugged off his hand and ran lightly down the stairs. 'I'll wait outside. Fix yourself something for dinner.'

She slammed the door behind her and stood on the doorstep, breasts heaving as she tried to calm herself. The nerve of the man. Blast him, anyway! Just who did he think he was? To set himself up as the arbitrator of whom she could go out with, whom she could have dinner with. It was fine for him to declare he wanted her, then go off and spend God knew how much time with Naomi, but if she just tried to go out once on a friendly outing with George, it was different. Stay home, Jenny, don't go out, as if he expected her to sit around awaiting his pleasure.

She was not growing calm, she was getting angrier by the minute. This would never do. She owed it to George to be in a pleasant mood when he arrived. It wasn't his fault that Kyle was so infuriating. Taking a deep breath, she deliberately stopped thinking of Kyle Martin and his autocratic ideas.

When George arrived, Jenny greeted him with a pleasant smile and settled back in his Mercedes to enjoy the drive. The trip to Lake Tahoe passed quickly as George kept the conversation general, his big car moving swiftly along the mountain roads.

Dinner was at the Del Webb's High Sierra Hotel, in the dining-room overlooking the lake.

'I wasn't sure you would join me tonight,' George said when they had ordered.

'Why not? You're pleasant company, and it's a delightful restaurant. I do like Lake Tahoe.'

'I'm glad. Actually, heard a rumour that you and Kyle were ... well, rather more than just cousins, shall I say.'

The colour stole into her cheeks as she dropped her eyes. She didn't know what to say. How had he heard that? She looked up at last. 'We don't really have a purely cousinly relationship. Kyle was Johnny's cousin.'

'But more than just—umm—kissing kin.'

'What do you mean?'

'Well, Nate seemed to think you two had something going. As I said, I'm glad you don't, that you were available to join me tonight.'

'I am, too.' She was puzzled. Jenny hadn't thought Nate and George were friends. Certainly not to the extent of talking about a couple found kissing on a blanket on a hillside.

'Kyle staying long?' George asked.

'He's convalescing from an accident, as you know. I think he plans to stay the whole summer. Until school starts in the fall.'

'I remember he mentioned a trip to Europe he had to miss. Teaches history?'

'That's right. Are you planning any trips soon? You know Susie is going to Hawaii for vacation? She's been saving for ages.' Jenny was uncomfortable with George's questions about Kyle. For some reason, which she found hard to define, she wanted to change the subject.

They talked about people they knew, different places they had visited. Jenny began to relax and enjoy the meal. The view was lovely, the lake was a deep blue, the sky gradually changing from light blue to pink to mauve, and finally the dark velvet black of the mountain night.

After the waiter had left their coffee, George again began to question Jenny on Kyle. She tried to think carefully before each response, but was worried with the line of conversation.

'Why is he staying with you? You didn't know each other before, did you?'

'Well, we had met before, of course.' That, at least, was true.

'But he and Johnny weren't close. Nate said he never saw him before.'

'Nate?' It must have been a lengthy conversation.

'Well, Nate knew a lot of Johnny's cousins. They were always running around together with Nick as kids. What do you know about this Kyle Martin?'

'Really, George, you sound as if you don't like Kyle,' she stalled.

'It's not that, Jenny.' He covered her hand with his, giving a light squeeze. 'I'm just worried about you, that's all. I feel sort of responsible for you.'

'I'm flattered, but I'm fine. Kyle is quite ... quite nice.' What an inadequate word, and inaccurate. She had never thought of him as nice. Exciting, perhaps, exasperating, infuriating, hard to understand. But not nice.

'He's not taking advantage, then.' George withdrew a little.

'No, of course not. Really, George, he's a perfect guest.'

'Out hiking a lot?'

'Not really. He's only starting to get about. We went for his first walk Sunday.' There was no point in trying to deny that, as George had obviously heard about it from Nate. Jenny continued to be puzzled: she really hadn't thought of Nate and George as friends. Her suspicion grew, but Jenny thrust it away. She would not suspect George.

'But Kyle was tired when we got home. I think we went too far for a first-time hike.' That would lend credence to the story-line they were following.

Taking a deep breath, Jenny looked directly at George. 'I didn't realise you and Nate were such friends.' There, let him make something out of that!

'We've known each other for years. I saw him this morning when I took the car in. Just idle talk, you know. Care for anything else?'

Jenny was glad when they started for home. She usually enjoyed her evenings with George Carlisle, but tonight she was disturbed. She wanted to talk to Kyle about the odd atmosphere over dinner. Surely George had questioned her more about Kyle than just normal curiosity would warrant? As they drove along, she tried to envision George engaging in idle chatter while someone repaired a car. It didn't seem like him, somehow.

When they reached her house, Jenny thanked him for the evening.

'I enjoyed myself, George.' She smiled at him. 'Want to come in for coffee?'

He glanced to the house, one light shining in the ground-floor window. 'No, not tonight, thanks. Let's do it again soon, Jenny.'

He leaned forward and kissed her gently on the mouth. Jenny sat still, assessing the kiss. She was shocked to discover nothing. It was as if she was kissing her grandfather, or Johnny's brother. George's lips were firm, slightly cool. She kissed him back just a little and then smiled.

'Goodnight.'

She watched as the car drove off, wondering what was wrong with her. If Kyle had kissed her, she would have gone up in smoke. But he was not available, while George was. Yet George was not able to make her senses stir, her heartbeat increase. It might be so simple if he could.

Kyle was stretched out on the sofa, watching TV. He looked up when she walked in, a scowl on his face.

'Hi,' Jenny said brightly.

'You're home early. Have a nice dinner?' He raised a sardonic eyebrow.

She flushed a little and moved to sit near the sofa on the chair.

'I had a lovely time,' she replied defiantly. 'Did you get some dinner?'

'Yes.' He turned back to the TV.

Jenny bit her lip, watching Kyle look at the TV. She had wanted to confide in him, tell him about the awkward conversation with George, not have it be like this. Would Kyle listen to her? Would he think it odd, or that she was just being fanciful?

'Kyle?'

'What?' His dark eyes looked at her under lowered brows. It was not an auspicious start.

'I—er—just wanted to talk. Are you watching the show?'

'Obviously I am, Jenny. If you want to talk, though, I'll turn it off.'

'Well, you don't have to, just listen. George questioned me a lot tonight, mostly about you.'

Kyle looked at her, a puzzled expression on his face. 'So? Probably doesn't like some man staying with you. I wouldn't.'

'Don't be silly, you're supposed to be Johnny's cousin.'

Kyle sat up and shook his head. 'Don't *you* be silly! We wouldn't be closely related, even if I were Johnny's cousin. You're a beautiful woman, what man who had any interest in you would want another man living with you?'

Jenny's eyes widened a little. No one, not even her mother, had ever called her beautiful before.

Did Kyle really think so? Then she frowned as the rest of what he'd said sank in.

'Well, you aren't really living with me.'

'Not my fault!' His mood lightened and the amusement she so often saw on his face was in evidence.

'Kyle, I want to talk about George.'

'Fine. Come sit here.' He patted the sofa beside him.

'I'm fine here.'

'I can hear better from here.'

Jenny paused for a moment, then hesitantly rose and sat beside him on the sofa.

'What did George ask to get you worried?'

'First, lots of questions about you: why you came here, if I'd met you before, things like that. Then he talked about Nate. Remember I told you I didn't think they were friends? Well, tonight he was repeating things Nate had told him.'

'You said they knew each other. Maybe they just met in town and talked.'

'Nate told him about meeting us the other day on the mountain. You don't just bring up things like that to casual acquaintances, do you?'

Kyle was silent a moment, then shook his head.

'So, what are you suggesting?'

'I don't know,' she said. 'Just an interesting connection, don't you think?'

'Yeah.' Kyle reached for her hand, lacing his fingers through hers and raising their hands to his lips, lightly touching each of her fingertips. 'Not as interesting as you, though.'

Jenny's hand tingled. The touch of his mouth on her fingers caused more feeling in her whole body than George's kiss had. The feel of Kyle's hard palm against hers was distracting, so that she couldn't concentrate.

'I think I'll try a new tactic,' he murmured, looking down at her.

'A new tactic?' Jenny said softly, conscious of his thumb gently rubbing the back of her hand. She opened her mouth a little to draw in air; she had trouble breathing, her stomach was filled with butterflies. Her eyes moved to his mouth, drawn there irresistibly.

Would Kyle kiss her again? The touch of his hand alone evoked emotions and feelings within her that George had never approached. She longed to feel his mouth on hers again.

'Where did you go for dinner?' Kyle asked, putting his feet up on the coffee table, resting their linked hands on his muscular thigh as he leaned back, his thumb still gently rubbing her soft skin.

Jenny found it hard to remember. 'We went to Lake Tahoe, the High Sierra.'

'I'm glad you didn't stay late.'

'Well, we ate, then drove back.'

'He didn't want to come in? Or didn't you ask him?'

'I did, but he said another time.' Jenny experimentally tried pulling back her hand, but he held it fast. 'Do you think it suspicious that George kept asking questions about you?'

'Do you?'

'Yes, I do. George isn't the type to ask questions like that ordinarily.' She was silent for a long moment, thinking, turning things over in her mind.

'Do you think he could be involved in the marijuana?'

Kyle shrugged. 'Too early to say. Right now almost anyone could be involved, or no one we've seen.'

Jenny was silent a minute, hoping it was someone she didn't know. She didn't want anyone in Palmer to be involved. She realised it was wishful thinking on her part, that things didn't always turn out the way someone wanted. Wishing didn't make it so.

She looked up at him when he tugged gently at her hand. His other hand came up to her neck, his fingers warm and caressing, tangling in the soft hair at her neckline. Slowly Kyle pulled her to him until they were only inches apart.

'I want you, Jenny,' he said softly, his eyes warm, gazing deep into hers, dark and hungry.

She stiffened and would have pulled back, but his hand was firm against her neck.

'Maybe not tonight, or even tomorrow. But soon, sweetheart, I'm going to have you.'

Her heart lurched with his words. For one sweet moment Jenny let her imagination run riot. To envisage lying with Kyle in a bed, feeling his body against hers, his hands on her, giving them both hours of pleasure.

She grew warm with the thought, the longing almost tangible. Then she shook her head to deny the dream, to deny him.

'Oh, yes, sweet Jenny, before I go.'

He brought his lips to hers, shifted on the sofa and released her hand to take her in his arms.

Whatever George had lacked, Kyle didn't. His mouth brought Jenny alive, his lips against hers, his tongue igniting the flame that consumed her. Her bones seemed to dissolve and turn to molten fire.

She reached to encircle his neck, bringing her soft breasts against his rock-hard chest, moving against him as she felt her breasts swell, grow firm. Kyle pulled her tightly against him, shifting again to lie on the sofa, Jenny following him down.

His tongue traced the soft inner lining of her mouth, rubbed her teeth, teased her tongue, invited it to follow to his mouth. She kissed him lingeringly, yearning for more, knowing the madness must stop soon.

His hands moulded her body to his, repositioning her to lie on top of him, his hands on her back, moving slowly to her waist, her hips, back along her spine. Jenny felt the desire in him rise, matched by the longing she felt. This was madness, sweet madness.

He pulled his mouth away to trail hot kisses along her jaw, to the warm pulse in her throat, up the column of her neck to her earlobe. Slowly he unzipped her dress, to find only a bra. She stiffened slightly when the zip moved.

'Relax,' he murmured lazily. 'I'm not going to do anything you don't want. I only want to touch you, feel your skin, not your dress.'

Placing his hands on her bare back, he traced her spine.

Jenny moved seductively against him, her body responding automatically to the slow rhythm of his touch. Kyle took her mouth again as his hands pressed her tighter to him. Her senses swam with blurred delight as his kiss deepened, thrilled, excited.

Kyle's hands rose to tangle themselves in Jenny's soft hair, moving her head back and forth as he drank deeply of the kisses she gave.

Then, with a ragged breath, he lifted her head.

She opened her eyes a little to gaze down at him.

'This is as far as I can go and not take you here and now. If you don't want to sleep with me tonight, you'd better get yourself upstairs right now,' he said, hoarsely.

Of course she wanted to sleep with him, tonight, tomorrow night, every night! Then sanity returned. There was a limit to the nights: it would be just until he left. He had said it himself.

Jenny's eyes widened and she scrambled up in confusion and shame. How could she have been a party to this? She wasn't as modern as she'd thought. She still believed in old-fashioned virtues.

She didn't consider herself a prude, but she did want more than casual sex, more than a few nights together, no matter how wonderful.

'Goodnight,' she mumbled, and fled for the stairs and the sanctity of her room.

CHAPTER TEN

THE next few days flew by. Kyle spent more and more time away from the house, not telling Jenny where he was going, no longer taking her with him. When she asked once or twice where he was going, he refused to tell her, saying only that it didn't concern her.

Jenny was embarrassed at first about the evening on the sofa, but Kyle made no mention of it, treating her as matter of factly as always, and soon she grew at ease with him again.

She wondered once or twice if he were seeing Naomi, but she didn't think that was the reason for his long absences. Naomi had her job in San Francisco and, unless on vacation, she would be there during the week.

On Saturday, Kyle asked Jenny to drive them to Strawberry. They met Stuart Brownley for lunch there. He had brought a motorcycle for Kyle's use.

'You aren't going to ride it, are you?' Jenny sounded horrified when she saw the big black Harley and realised what its purpose was.

'Of course, you don't think it'll get itself to your place, do you?' Kyle asked.

'But your arm! You shouldn't be driving around on that machine. It's not safe.'

'It's fine. Good transportation around here, and easily hidden. Don't fret, Jenny,' he said impatiently.

Stuart Brownley turned to hide his smile at their exchange.

They ate lunch at the local café. Stuart and Kyle talked shop, Stuart bringing Kyle up to date on different assignments others in their group were working on. He started to say something once about Kyle's assignment, but Kyle stopped him.

'Later.' He glanced at Jenny.

'I'm not going to tell anyone,' she said indignantly.

'I know, but I like to operate on the need-to-know basis. You don't need to know. Besides, you have a very expressive face. I don't want you to inadvertently give something away.'

Jenny glared at him and Stuart, turning away in disdain when both men roared with laughter at her look.

After lunch they walked Jenny back to her truck, Kyle opening the door for her.

'I'm going to go over some things with Stuart. I'll be back for dinner.'

Jenny, still annoyed with the laughter at lunch, nodded stiffly and put the key in the ignition.

'Don't sulk, baby.' Kyle leaned in the cab to turn her head, giving her a quick kiss. He then slammed the door.

She met the amused look on Stuart's face, and blushed. Darting a quick glance at Kyle, she nodded again.

'OK. Drive carefully on that fool bike,' she said.

It was the first time he'd touched her since their night on the sofa. She ran her tongue lightly around her lips, wishing he'd kiss her again. Impatiently she jerked her thoughts back. He was not for her.

When he arrived home in the late afternoon, Kyle was preoccupied. He ate dinner quickly, then retired to the den, pulling the phone in from the hall and closing the door. He spent the evening there, on the phone. Jenny could hear the murmur of his voice as she went up to bed.

With the advent of the motorcycle, Jenny scarcely saw Kyle. He left the house early each day, often before she was up and dressed. If he stayed for breakfast, he'd bolt as soon as it was finished. In the evenings, Jenny was usually in bed when the muffled roar of the big Harley announced his return.

Jenny felt shut out. She recognised why Kyle operated under the need-to-know theory, and his reservations of telling her everything but, after all, she was providing him a base of operation, had provided the background information he needed for the assignment. To be totally excluded from the project now hurt.

Did Kyle feel her usefulness was at an end? Maybe she could still help. If she could provide some further assistance, maybe Kyle would take her into his confidence, know she could be trusted, spend more time with her. And she knew exactly what would help, too.

Going into the den, Jenny looked for the topographical map he had used. If she could locate the marijuana field on it, identify the fire road that ran by it, she'd have something to offer.

The map wasn't in the den. After only a moment's indecision, Jenny went up to Kyle's room. It must be there. The door was open and she walked boldly in. Traces of his aftershave lingered in the air and she stopped for a moment, almost feeling his presence.

There was a stack of papers on the dresser. She rifled through them, finding the map; poring over it, trying to pinpoint where her house was located, the way they had walked through the hills and where the field might be.

She found a couple of possibilities, and both near a fire road. The next step was to drive out and see. Telling Shasta to guard the house, she went for her truck.

Once on the dirt road of the fire trails, Jenny drove slowly, carefully. She kept a close watch in her rear-view mirror, to make sure she wasn't being followed. If this was the correct road, she had no desire to be found on it by the growers.

Jenny had marked on the map where she thought the field was, and she tried to equate what she saw with what was on the map. Twice she stopped, climbed out and scouted along the north side of the road. She hadn't seen the road, Kyle had, on his tour through the trees, but she knew the field was on the north side, not too far from the road. She drove further, stopping again.

She pushed her way through a small rim of trees, and burst through to the marijuana field. She'd found it! It lay before her gently sloping upward, silent in the hot sun.

Wait until she told Kyle! She smiled, picturing his face when she informed him of her discovery.

'What the hell are you doing here?' Kyle's angry face blazed down at her. Glancing over her shoulder towards the road, his face, tight, he turned back to Jenny. 'If you've messed up this bust, I'll bust you!' His voice was harsh, his features taut with anger.

Two men came silently out of the shadows from the perimeter. One walked warily, the other had a big grin on his face. Jenny recognised him as Jason Sperry from Kyle's office.

'Mac, drive the truck this lady came in up the road about a mile, try to find a hiding place. You come with me.' Kyle jerked her arm.

Jenny stumbled, then recovered as she tried to match his long stride.

'Your dumb old bust is fine. No one followed me,' she grumbled, overcoming her surprise at seeing him. So much for trying to surprise him with the discovery of the field from the road! He had beaten her to it.

'Not on the road, maybe. But you don't know whether they come by that road. Duck down.'

They crouched down and entered a thicket of scrub, madrone, cottonwood and mesquite. Blankets, food and camera gear were carefully stacked to one side.

'What's this?' Jenny asked in surprise.

'A stake-out. Why are you here, Jenny? What's going on?' Kyle's voice was heavy, ominous.

Jason followed them in, picked up the camera again, and smiled at Jenny. 'Hi,' he said.

'Hi, Jason.' Jenny stalled.

Kyle recognised it. 'Jenny!'

'I was trying to find the road, so I could tell you, help you out. I didn't know you already knew about it. I was only trying to help.'

His face softened just a little as he shook his head. 'If I'd known you'd try a fool thing like this, I'd have told you.'

'I know, the need-to-know principle.'

Jason threw her a quick grin. 'Kyle's favourite axiom.'

'Watch the field,' Kyle said drily.

'At least now I understand why you asked for this assignment,' Jason murmured irrepressibly, turning back to the field, camera held ready.

Jenny looked puzzled for a moment, then turned back to Kyle, her voice low.

'Why are you doing a stake-out now? I thought you were going to catch them when harvesting.'

'Change of plan. We want to destroy this field now, before harvest. If we can get a line on who's interested in it now, and a few pictures, we'll arrest and destroy now. Sooner or later someone has to come to turn on the water for a little while. My guess is soon. The plants are starting to wilt a little already in the heat. Once they come, we'll snap their pictures and wrap it up.'

'Catch them in the act.'

'Right.'

Jenny sat quietly, thinking through the implication of his comment. If they accomplished it soon, Kyle would be leaving soon. While she had known he wouldn't stay for ever, she had thought he'd stay until late summer, until the marijuana field was harvested. Now, it could all be over soon, in days, not weeks. She caught her breath, as a small dart of pain penetrated her. She had known his being here was temporary, but she had thought she had more time. It was ending too soon.

She glanced at him under her lashes, remembering he'd said he'd sleep with her before he left. Had he meant it? Did he remember, too? She looked at her hands. Did she want him to? She was not one for an affair, but would it come to that?

One night of ecstasy, it would be a memory to last her all her life. Was it worth it? She took a deep breath. Time would go so fast.

'How long have you been here?'

'Since Stuart brought me the bike. Jason and Mac are staying in Strawberry.'

'But only to sleep,' Jason grumbled quietly. 'We're here from dawn till ten or so every night. Don't know when they'll come to check on their precious crop. I wish they'd hurry up. We'll get them when they do.'

Jenny looked again at Kyle. His brooding gaze was on her. Nervously she looked away.

'Now what?'

'You can stay here for a little while, with us. You wanted to find it, now you have.'

Jenny refused to look at Kyle. He was angry she'd come. If she had known that would be his reaction to her attempt to help, she wouldn't have tried. She didn't want to make him angry. Squirming back to lean against a tree, she tried to relax.

It was peaceful in the thicket, sheltered from the hot sun—quiet and restful. A slow contentment gradually stole over her.

Once or twice during the afternoon, Jason glanced over to Kyle or Jenny, then back to the field, camera always ready to go. Mac was hidden part way up the hillside, ready to signal if the growers came from another direction. They didn't talk, just watched.

Jenny refrained from looking at Kyle after her first two tries. His eyes bore into hers, his look unfathomable. Still, she found pleasure in being with him, just being near him.

'Hey, Kyle, when Jenny leaves, go with her and bring back some burgers. I'd love to have something hot to eat for a change,' Jason said softly as the afternoon waned.

'And just how do you propose I get back, without turning the road into a damn freeway?'

'Take a chance?' Jason offered half-heartedly.

'You could hike back from my place,' Jenny said. 'I have an insulated carry-all that'll keep the food hot.'

'You're an angel!' Jason said fervently.

'Sure, easy for you to say,' Kyle remarked drily. 'You don't have to carry it. OK, OK, I'll do it. Let's go.' Kyle stood as much as the confined space would allow and led the way out.

'I want everything on it,' Jason called softly.

Jenny rose to follow, smiling. 'Bye, Jason.'

'Bye, Jenny. See you again some time.'

She nodded and followed Kyle. He stayed near the trees, working his way up to Mac.

'We're going for dinner. Where did you put the truck?'

Mac tossed him the keys. 'About a mile and a half up on the left, a nice culvert, by a tall cedar.'

'We'll find it. Hamburgers OK?'

'Sounds good. I like everything on it.'

'Right. I'll be hiking back from that direction.' Kyle pointed to the east.

Working their way back along the perimeter to the road, Kyle paused and looked carefully before they stepped out to the dusty dirt fire trail. Trudging along, Jenny watched his profile as he walked a step or two ahead of her.

'I'm sorry,' she said slowly. 'I see now I could have ruined everything. But honestly, I thought it'd be a good surprise for you.'

Kyle stopped and looked at her, then looked back down the road. He reached out and drew Jenny to his chest, looking down at her upturned face. Slowly his head bent and he kissed her.

'I've been wanting to do that all afternoon,' he said against her lips, his breath intermingling with hers, soft kisses accenting each word.

Reluctantly, slowly, he set her back with a sigh. 'But this isn't the time nor the place. Come on, let's find the blasted truck.'

Jenny smiled to herself as she hurried to keep up with his longer stride. It was as good as she remembered. She would miss him so much when he'd gone.

Jenny was cooking the hamburgers for Kyle to take back with him when the phone rang.

'I'll get it for you.' Kyle rose from the table where he'd been watching her and moved down the hall. Jenny put down the condiments and moved to the door, wondering who was calling.

'No, I can't make it tonight, I already have plans, but tomorrow would be good for me. How about you?' Kyle said into the phone. He listened for a moment then finished, 'Fine, I'll pick you up at seven.'

Jenny stared at him as the penny dropped. 'Naomi?' she hazarded as he turned from the phone.

'Yes. She's up for the weekend again. I'll see her tomorrow.'

Jenny turned and went back to the stove. Carefully she turned the burgers, and prepared the buns. She would not let him know how much disappointment she felt after his simple statement. All week he'd left her alone, with no explanation, and then Naomi called and he dropped everything to be with her. Jenny wouldn't be expressive and have him guess how she felt, however. She only had to hold it in for a little longer, just until he left.

'There are sodas in the fridge,' she said brightly, 'I'll run up and get the insulated bag.'

She fled the room and hurried up the stairs, tears sparkling in her eyes. She dashed them away and retrieved the bag from the hall cupboard. Taking a deep steadying breath, she pasted a smile on her face and went back downstairs.

When the meal was packed, she handed him the carry-all with a bright smile, one which did not reach her eyes.

'Are you all right?' Kyle asked, pausing before he left.

'Sure, have fun. Thanks for letting me sit in on part of the stake-out, I've never done that before.' She looked only as high as his chin.

He leaned down to kiss her lightly, but Jenny refused to meet his eyes, stood stoically, holding her breath, wishing for the moment to end, for him to leave, only wanting to be alone.

'I'll be back,' he said, leaving by the back door.

Jenny turned to watch him go, his tall body moving easily, his long stride covering the ground rapidly.

She hugged herself tightly, trying to ease the ache in her heart, as her eyes filled and her throat grew tight. She'd known all along he wasn't for her, but it still hurt. She loved him. She knew that now, for all the good it did her. Loved him as she had Johnny. No, differently from Johnny, but none the less stronger or lasting for being a second love. A last love.

Like her first love, one that she couldn't have. Sadly she watched him out of sight, then turned and walked blindly up the stairs as the tears spilled over and ran down her face.

Jenny stayed in her room the next morning until she heard his motorcycle leave. It was late when she ventured forth, but she hadn't wanted to see Kyle. After she had eaten, she called Susie.

'How about going to the river? We can lie in the sun and swim.'

'Good idea. I'll bring a lunch. Want to go into Strawberry tonight? That new Burt Reynolds movie is playing.'

'Yes, that'll be fun. We can eat dinner there, too. Make a day of it. I'll drop Shasta off at my folks' after the river, then pick him up after the film.'

'Is Kyle coming too?' Susie asked.

'No, he's busy today.' Jenny scarcely felt a pang as she said it. Maybe she could get over him, learn to go on as before. She hadn't known him for long. Long enough, her heart reminded her.

Arranging to pick Susie up at her place, Jenny hung up.

Glad to have Susie's company for the day, Jenny hurried to get ready. She wished she could confide fully in her friend, but to do so would blow Kyle's cover and maybe endanger his assignment. She wouldn't let personal concerns threaten the assignment. He could trust her!

Besides, Susie would probably advise Jenny to take what was offered while the going was good, and worry about the future tomorrow. Susie and Jenny were friends, but their outlooks had always differed.

It was therapeutic lying in the hot sun beside a tributary to the American River. When they got hot they would plunge into the icy water, swim until they were cold, then climb out to bake again in the sun.

The film was entertaining, though Jenny found herself speculating as to where Kyle and Naomi were, and what they might be doing. Again and again she had to drag her attention back to the film.

After dropping Susie off, Jenny went to her parents' home to pick up Shasta.

'Did you enjoy the movie?' her father asked when she came in.

'Yes, it's funny. Burt is good in roles like that. Hi, Shasta, ready to go home?'

'Stay for some cocoa, honey,' her mother offered, rising to prepare it.

Jenny smiled. 'Sounds good. I'll help.'

She followed her mother into the kitchen, and got down the cups while her mother put the milk on the stove to warm.

'Why don't you and Kyle come to dinner tomorrow?' Peggy O'Neil said while they waited for the milk to heat. 'We've only met him, and I used to know Edith so well.'

'Kyle is seeing Naomi Taylor,' Jenny said carefully, rearranging the cups on the counter. 'I don't know if he's planning to see her tomorrow or not. But I'd love to come, Mom.'

'Ask Naomi, too, if you want. I haven't seen much of her since she went to San Francisco. She looked washed out at George's affair. Too many late nights, I guess.'

Jenny looked at her mother closely. She had thought Naomi looked rather great.

'Well, I'll ask them. I'd like to come, anyway.'

'We liked Kyle. Your father only met him the night he ran out of gas, but we chatted the other afternoon, plus I spoke with him at George's party. He's a fine man.'

Jenny carried her cup carefully, happy her mother liked Kyle, wishing . . .

Jenny stayed later than she had planned to, discussing George Carlisle's party, the new display her father was planning in his store, her mother's plans to enter the flower contest at the county fair in August. It was after midnight when Jenny and Shasta climbed into the truck and started for home.

As she drew near her driveway a single headlight came up behind her, and settled to follow her. Turning into her drive, she knew it was Kyle. Her spirits rose. At least he hadn't stayed the night with Naomi.

He pulled his motorcycle into the garage beside her, waiting at the rear of the truck for her to join him.

'Date with George?' he asked silkily as she headed for the house.

'Maybe,' she prevaricated. 'Have fun with Naomi?'

'It was interesting. Where have you been?'

Jenny unlocked the door, switched on the lights. As Kyle stepped closer, she caught a whiff of the perfume Naomi used so lavishly.

'I've been out, now I'm back,' she said, and ran up the stairs. She paused at the top to look back at Kyle, standing just inside the door.

'My mother's invited us for dinner tomorrow, can you go?'

He nodded.

'About seven.'

Jenny turned and fled to her room.

She ached with longing for the man—what was wrong with her? As she crawled between her sheets she tried to block out the images her mind conjured. Kyle last winter, his pallor earlier this summer, kisses on the hillside, in the hall, carrying her to bed after the party, their encounter on the sofa. She tried to remember he was making a play for Naomi, and considered her, Jenny, only a perk to this job. Once the job was over, he'd be gone. She tried to remember, but to no avail. She wanted him as much as he wanted her, she ached with desire, longing. Yearned to feel his lips against hers again, the rising delight he could evoke with his touch. She loved him. What was she going to do?

CHAPTER ELEVEN

JENNY didn't see Kyle again until it was time to leave for her parents' home the next day. She wore a short, white-dotted Swiss dress which buttoned down the front, and white sandals. Her tan had deepened from the day at the river and the white showed it to advantage. Her hair curled and waved, new golden highlights from the sun brightening it.

Kyle was downstairs when she went down. He wore the designer jeans he'd worn to George's barbecue, and a white cotton turtle-neck sweater. His eyes flashed momentarily when he saw her, then he turned away.

'Ready?' she said nervously. It wasn't fair he should look so virile, so sexy. What chance did she have?

'Yes. Are we taking Shasta?'

'No.'

They drove to town in silence, Jenny paying strict attention to the road, Kyle gazing out the window.

'Hi, Jenny.' Her mother gave her a brief kiss when they arrived. 'Hi, Kyle, so glad you could join us.' Peggy O'Neil looked beyond them. 'Naomi not able to make it?'

Kyle slanted a sardonic look at Jenny, then smoothly replied, 'No, she drove back to San Francisco this afternoon.'

'You remember Dan?'

Kyle shook hands warmly with Jenny's father. 'Good to see you again.'

'Come in. Actually, come on through to the back-yard, we're grilling steaks there. Can I get you something to drink, Kyle? Jenny?'

'Gin and tonic, please.'

'Me, too,' Jenny said, giving her father a hug.

'Tell me all about what Edith's doing these days.' Peggy said to Kyle when they were seated and drinks dispersed. 'She and I were best of friends as girls, then we drifted apart. I haven't heard from her in ages.'

'She's not a very good correspondent,' Kyle acknowledged with a grin. 'She travels a lot, you know.' He glanced at Jenny as if to say, join in at any time.

'Didn't you say she was in Texas touring the Alamo?' She helped out, grinning a little at his discomfort.

'Yes, she wanted to stand where Davy Crockett stood.'

'That sounds just like Edith.' Peggy sighed. 'Next time you see her, tell her to give me a call. I never knew your father. She ran off with the first man right after high school. Divorced him before she was twenty. She must have married your father right away. How old are you, Kyle?'

He took a swallow of his drink, rapidly calculating.

'Twenty-eight.'

Jenny's eyes widened at that, and she quickly glanced at her parents for their reaction. Peggy nodded.

'That'd fit then, Jenny's twenty-five. How long was Edith married to your father?'

'Not long,' Kyle hedged.

Jenny was getting concerned. Any minute now her mother would ask something Kyle wouldn't know and he'd blow the whole thing. She wasn't sure how to turn the subject without her mother becoming suspicious. Oh, well, she'd have to try.

'Mother, tell Kyle about entering the flower contest at the fair this year,' Jenny said brightly.

Her parents both looked at her, rather oddly she thought, but maybe it was guilty conscience. Kyle's face creased in amusement as he gave her a deliberate wink.

'For best of variety or as an arrangement?' he asked, taking Jenny's lead.

Once or twice during the evening Jenny would look up to find her mother's eyes on her or Kyle rather speculatively. Jenny would smile awkwardly, glance to Kyle and then back to her food.

As the evening wore on, they shifted seats, moving away from the table to take their coffee and brandy. They sat long after dark fell, sipping the beverages, talking. Under cover of darkness, Kyle reached for Jenny's hand, holding it lightly on his thigh, caressing it absently now and again.

Jenny didn't think her parents could see him holding her hand. If so, what would they think after she'd told them Kyle was interested in Naomi Taylor? She certainly didn't want to give her mother any romantic ideas.

She enjoyed the evening. Her parents were relaxed and amusing in the topics of conversation they chose. Kyle fitted in well and Jenny could tell that both her parents liked him. Of Kyle she was less sure. How much was genuine, how much a part of the act?

She was always questioning that. Just when she was feeling comfortable, doubt would creep in: how much was Kyle on duty and how much was Kyle the man?

Jenny felt bereft when it was time to depart and he let her hand go.

'I'll drive back, shall I?' he asked after bidding her parents farewell.

'That would be nice.' Jenny didn't like driving at night.

The moon rose high in the sky, casting a silvery glow, deep shadows, as they drove through the night, the headlights of the truck thrusting bold slashes of light. Kyle drove swiftly, competently. Jenny rested her head against the seat-back, watching him from the faint glow of the dashboard, his hair falling on his forehead, the strong jawline, the way his hands held the wheel.

He stopped the truck before the house, switched off the lights and engine. 'Your parents are nice. They'd make good friends.'

'I'm glad you think so.'

The light from the moon enabled her to see him, though not clearly. Reluctantly, she got out of the truck.

When she opened the front door to the house, he stopped her as she reached for the lights.

'There's plenty of light from the moon, we don't need the electric ones.'

His breath smelled slightly of brandy as he pulled her into his arms. Jenny moved closer and put her arms around him, tilting her face for his kiss.

He held back for a moment, gazing down at her in the silvery moonlight before slowly lowering his mouth to hers.

Kyle's touch exploded her senses, setting her afloat on a sea of delight. When his mouth moved to her neck, her throat, she arched against him, moving her head back to better receive his kisses.

With a muffled groan he swept her up in his arms and turned to mount the stairs. Jenny, conscious of his injury, took as much of her weight as she could, kissing Kyle's ear, teasing the lobe with her tongue, moving to meet his hot mouth when he turned to her.

He laid her on his bed, immediately following her down, his mouth a sweet, hot focal point until his hands began their caressing assault. He laced the fingers of her two hands through one of his and drew them over her head. His mouth hot and sweet against hers, she opened fully to receive him and met his demands as her tongue answered his, her lips moving against his.

When he slowly opened the buttons of her dress, his fingers found the satin of her skin.

'You aren't wearing a bra?' He raised up a little to look down at her, as the moonlight illuminated his room in a silvery glow.

She shook her head slowly on the pillow, her soft, brown hair spread out about her, a smile playing around her mouth as she strained to see him clearly. His touch was light, feathering as his fingertips skimmed over her fevered flesh, his eyes watching as his hands roamed over her, learned her, from neck to shoulder, down over one breast, pausing to circle lightly one rosy tip before plunging into the valley between, drifting up to lightly circle the other tip.

Jenny shivered beneath his touch, mesmerised by it, straining to see his expression in the faint illumination, absorbing the delight of his touch, yearning for more.

He continued with the buttons until the dress was undone. Spreading the faint material, his hand continued its exploration, down her abdomen, his knuckle gently grazing her navel, moving lower to caress the firm flesh of her thighs, dropping between them to slowly, slowly draw his fingers up against her.

'Oh, Kyle,' she moaned, yearning for more, wanting his mouth against hers, wanting him to assuage the aching he was building within her.

Still holding her hands above her head, he bent to kiss one swelling breast, to flick and tease her nipple with his hot tongue, gently suck the hard tip, pulling and teasing as Jenny began to move against the hot waves he caused.

When she was breathless, Kyle moved to the other breast, his mouth taking the sweetness there as his fingers continued moving against her abdomen, to her thighs, between, back up, so slowly, so tantalising.

'Kyle, please,' she whispered hoarsely. She didn't ever remember feeling so senseless, so sensuous, so crazed with desire. Her body was on fire, a slow, pulsing throbbing, demanding to be met.

She moved against his touch, arching to his fingers, moving against his mouth, offering her breast more fully, wanting more from him. She tried to pull down her hands, to draw him to her, but he held them firmly.

'Kyle, please!' she begged.

'Say it, Jenny,' he demanded, drawing back a little, his fingers still trailing fire along her softness. 'Say you want me,' he commanded.

'I do, Kyle. I want you, please!' She was on fire for him, her whole being caught up in his touch, in his caresses and the fiery kisses he gave.

He kissed her swiftly and sat up, drawing his shirt over his head, tossing it on the floor. In two swift moves he withdrew his boots and lay back down, drawing Jenny against the hardness of his bare warm chest, his hands roaming over her as he drew her dress from her.

She fumbled with his jeans, anxious to remove them, to let body touch body, to meet unrestricted and unencumbered.

'Easy, baby,' he soothed her. 'We've got all the time we want.' He helped her unfasten his jeans, raising himself to take them off.

Shyly, Jenny ran her hands over him, pausing a moment when making contact with his scar, moving on as the heat built again within her.

He eased off her panties and rolled her on to her back. As he took one nipple gently between his teeth, his hand again moved to find her softness, to gently spread her legs. Jenny gave a soft moan as the touch of his fingers against her drove all thought from her mind. She could only feel Kyle, long for him. Love him.

Jenny arched to meet him when he covered her, arched again to receive him deep within her body. He moved his hand to cover her hips, to move her to the rhythm he wanted, to the tempo that was building up between them.

Slowly the fire burned, raging hotter and hotter until Jenny thought she was lost in the conflagration.

Suddenly wave after wave of molten pleasure spread through her body, each hotter and higher than the previous one until one final shattering wave broke, leaving her drained, breathless, complete, deliciously satisfied, satiated.

Their feverish movement slowed as the last wave burned itself out, leaving warmth and peace behind.

Jenny's breathing was erratic, fast. She could feel Kyle's the same. Holding him close, she rested her cheek against his, lassitude spreading rapidly as she enjoyed the weight of the man on her, the feel of him against her legs, her breasts, beneath her hands. She imprinted each sensation on her brain, to remember always.

Kyle raised his head, sought and found her mouth. He kissed her, kissed her again, rubbed his lips across her.

'You're good, Jenny, you're so good,' he said softly, moving to kiss her cheeks, her jaw, back to her mouth.

Compared to whom? she thought with a shock. What had she done? How could she have allowed herself to be taken in with brandy and moonlight?

She loved him, loved Kyle Martin with all of her being, yet knew he was not for her. He'd never even said he liked her. Fat, hot, slow tears welled up in her eyes, and spilled over. She'd have her one night, but was it worth it? And then what?

Kyle drew back. 'What's the matter?' One finger brushed her eye, wiped away a tear. 'Did I hurt you? Jenny, I didn't mean to. I wouldn't do anything to hurt you, sweetheart.'

She looked up at him, his image swimming in the tears.

'No, I'm fine,' she whispered. It was too late to turn back. Too late to undo what they'd done, she would go on.

She loved him so much that she ached with it. His face was shadowed, she could only just make it out in the silvery moonlight, but hers softened just knowing he was there. For whatever time they had, she'd cherish it. There was no other choice.

He rolled over on his back, bringing her to lie against his chest. Jenny rested her cheek against his shoulder, felt the rough scar tissue. Turning her head slightly, she kissed the place, then rested her cheek against it once more.

'Does it hurt?' she murmured.

'No, you kissed and made it better,' his voice rumbled in her ear, amusement evident in his tone.

He drew the sheet over them as the cool night air chilled their overheated bodies. As he held her in the circle of his arms, Jenny felt his mouth on her hair once or twice as she slowly drifted on the lassitude left from their lovemaking. Just before she dropped off, she remembered.

'Are you really twenty-eight?' she asked sleepily.

'No, I'm almost thirty-five. Years older than you, baby.'

'Mmm.' She snuggled closer, taking in the scent of his cologne, the male smell that was specially Kyle. Giving into the tiredness, she slept.

Kyle woke her in the night to make love. It was better than before and Jenny thought she had gone to heaven. Just before dawn he kissed her and told her goodbye, he had to go.

It was late when Jenny awoke to the day, bright sunlight flooding the room. She stretched languorously in the bed, putting her arms where Kyle had slept, dreamily reliving the previous night. His touch exhilarated, inflamed. The delightful pleasure he had brought her was wondrous. She wished he had not gone to his stake-out, but had stayed with her and made love to her all day.

She rolled on to her back, eyes wide, staring at the ceiling. As she became fully awake, sanity and common sense returned. It should not happen again. But could she see that it didn't? It had been wonderful, would always be wonderful with Kyle. But she couldn't let it happen again.

She sat up, confused, ashamed. What was she to do? Maybe she should suggest he leave, not be part of the temptation she was unable to refuse. But could she do that, deliberately send him from her life? He'd be gone soon enough. Too soon. She loved him so much, wanted to be with him as much as she could. How could she deliberately shorten their time together?

The day dragged by. Jenny caught herself daydreaming about last night, about a future which would hold only her and Kyle, one with no problems, no conflict, just the two of them. Each time she realised what she was doing, she would plunge furiously into work, only to find her mind drifting again, daydreaming again.

What she needed to decide was how to handle their next encounter. Should she play it cool? Or be angry? Looking again at the clock, she wished the day would go faster so he'd be back home. She'd know how to react when she saw him.

When Kyle had not returned by dinner, Jenny knew he was on the stake-out, probably eating sandwiches and Cokes. Was he thinking of her? As the evening wore on, however, she fretted with impatience, waiting for his return, longing to see him. Anxiously she listened for the growl of the motorcycle, watched for a sign from Shasta that someone was coming. But the evening was quiet, the dog lay peaceably nearby.

It was after eleven before Jenny gave up and climbed the stairs to bed. She lay awake long into the night, still listening for the motorcycle. In vain. Kyle had not returned by the time she finally went to sleep shortly before dawn.

Jenny checked Kyle's room first thing when she awoke the next morning, but he hadn't returned. The bed was still tumbled from her hasty departure the day before, the table askew. The picture lay face down near the bed, its glass shattered. Had she jarred the table in her haste to leave yesterday, and knocked it off? She picked it up and placed it on the table, picking up the broken glass. She gazed down at the happy girl in the photo. What could she tell Jenny about Kyle?

On the off-chance that history repeated itself, Jenny closed the door and went to call her mother.

The last time he had not come in, he had stayed there. There was no truck with a faulty fuel gauge this time, he had his motorcycle. Still, she'd try, maybe something had happened.

'Hi, mom, we had a nice time on Sunday night.' That was more true than her mother knew!

'I'm glad, honey. We really like Kyle. Let's do it again soon. Are you coming into town today?'

'Yes, I've some of the accounts for Joe, and need to get some more work.'

'Want to stop by for lunch? You dad's gone down to Sacramento and I'm lonesome.'

'No, I'd better not. I've lots to do. Maybe tomorrow?' She hung up slowly, disappointment seeping into her. He had not stayed there. Where was he?

She could not see her mother today, for she would know instantly that something was wrong and question Jenny to find out what it was. Jenny wasn't ready to confide in her mother yet, though one day she might.

Where was he? Was he all right? Was Kyle at the stake-out, bored and restless with the vigil? Was he thinking of her at all? Wishing he could be with her as much as she was wishing he was with her? She loved him so, was it possible he could grow to love her? Naomi was work and she was a perk . . . could it be changed?

Had he left? Jenny's heart plunged with the thought, and she grew cold all over. Was that why he'd slept with her, because he was leaving? He had said he would do so before he left. Was that all that night had meant to him?

Jenny paced the hall, indecision, uncertainty and worry coursing through her. Her mind was in turmoil, her thoughts tumbled.

What if he'd been injured again? For a moment Jenny stopped short. How was she to know what was happening at the field? If the drug growers were dangerous, and were cornered, would they fight?

The vision of cowboy fights, guns blazing, dust puffing up filled her mind.

'Well, this is ridiculous!' she said to Shasta. 'Wondering won't get me answers. Come on, boy, we'll go find out.'

Grabbing her purse and keys, she hurried to the truck. As she pulled out of the drive, she reflected on the fact Kyle would probably be angry that she was coming, worried about alerting the growers, scaring them off. Well, she'd be careful, make sure no one was around when she went on the dirt road.

It was only minutes later that Jenny slowed for the turn, slowed, then sped up and passed it as she saw a black sedan turn in ahead of her.

Her heart beating faster, Jenny tried to see who was in the car. She didn't recognise anyone. She licked suddenly dry lips. Perhaps they were the drug growers. Oh, Kyle, be safe, she prayed. Fear of ruining the whole deal after so many weeks of planning caused her to turn around and return home.

She went through the rest of the morning doing what needed to be done, glad she had some work to do to occupy her mind, trying not to think of what might be happening. She almost went back to the stake-out, but knew he would be angry with her if she did, so she stayed away. Waiting was so hard!

In the early afternoon Jenny drove into town to exchange her completed work for new assignments, coming straight back home. As she drove the truck into the garage her mind dully noted that the motorcycle still hadn't returned.

Jenny went inside, dumping her work in the den, walking aimlessly around. There must be something she could do, some way to find out what was happening. Just sitting around was intolerable!

Brownley! She'd try Stuart Brownley, he should know if something were happening. He'd be able to advise her on what to do.

It only took a minute to find his number and place the call. She tapped her fingers on the table as it rang at the other end.

'Stuart Brownley, please,' she said when the phone was answered.

'He's out of the office for the day. Can anyone else help you?' The girl sounded young and friendly.

'Do you know where he is?' Jenny hadn't counted on his not being available. Did he know what was going on? Was he here in Palmer?

'No, I don't. I expect him back tomorrow. Can I have him call?'

'No, thanks.' If she didn't hear from Kyle before then, she would call back.

Slowly Jenny hung up the phone. She was growing sick with worry. Was he safe? Where was he?

She sank slowly to the chair, her eyes unseeing. Fear clutched her as she thought of the dangers Kyle faced daily. How did he do it? It was too much to bear. Why didn't he get a nice, safe, secure job, like being an accountant? A job that would not expose him to danger. Would he ever change, ever look for a safer occupation?

Hugging her arms tightly against her chest, Jenny tried to ease the fear that lodged there. Please God, let him be safe.

She took a deep breath. She couldn't continue like this, she must go on. She stood and started for the stairs. She'd go up and make his bed. No reason to leave it all messed up. Maybe tidy his room, then take Shasta for a walk. Not, however, to the marijuana field, but in the opposite direction. Kyle might not be back for hours yet. She dared not let her mind hold any other thoughts.

She went slowly up the stairs, opened his door.

Kyle was sitting on the edge of his bed, bent over the broken picture, holding it gently in his hands, a look of sadness on his face.

'Oh!' Jenny cried seeing him unexpectedly. He was safe! Thank God. The relief was almost overwhelming, her knees felt weak, her head light. He was safe and totally unaware of the anxiety and worry she had gone through. And so he must remain. It would never do to let him know how afraid she'd been for him. There was nothing to bind him to her, only her to him for ever by the love she had for Kyle. But he mustn't know.

'Jenny?' He looked up at her.

She slammed the door and turned down the hall. She was glad he was safe, oh, so glad, but knew she'd give herself away if she stayed another minute. She'd be OK in a few moments, she could get her emotions under control and face him. But not just yet. Her heart sang with relief at his presence, her mind sought a hiding place.

'Jenny!' Kyle caught her on the top step, his hand under her arm. 'What's wrong with you?' He drew her back into the hall, turned her to face him, a hand on each of her arms. 'What's the matter?'

Tears welling, the ache in her heart almost intolerable, she stared dumbly at him, shaking her head.

'Nothing!' She held her breath, but the tears spilled over, trailed down her cheeks. Dumbly she tried to stop, but couldn't.

'Come on, Jenny, sweetheart,' Kyle wiped one tear from her cheek. 'This is not nothing. What's the matter?'

The softness in his voice, the warm concern in his eyes were her undoing. It was as if the dam broke as the torrent of words spilled forth.

'I was so worried about you—you didn't come and weren't at Mom's and Brownley wasn't in and—and I saw the black car—and was afraid of guns.' She took a shaky breath before she spoke again. 'I hate your job, the danger you're in—hate that you expose yourself to risks every time you go out the door—how can you stand it? I hate the whole damn mess!' She collapsed against him, tears flowing, racking sobs shaking her whole body.

His arms came up to her back as he gently rocked her. 'Hey, what's going on? I've already had my shower, you know.'

She felt the warm skin of his chest against her cheek, he was clad only in his jeans. The feel of his hard chest against her skin was soothing. She gulped back a sob, able to hear the steady thud of his heart.

'Oh, Kyle, I'm so unhappy!' Tears flowed again. What was going to happen to them? She loved him so much! How could she ever bear to be parted?

'I can see that, baby, but I don't know why. I don't want you to be unhappy, I want you to be happy. I'm all right, and the job's over.'

She rested her head against him, closed her eyes, wishing this moment could go on for ever, never having to think, never having to face him again, just stay in the warm circle of his arms, float away into eternity. Her hands moved restlessly against his back, feeling the muscles ripple as he moved.

'Hey, Jenny, sweet, you can't do that if we're going to stand around all day. You've got to tell me what's wrong.'

She shook her head, another sob shaking her body.

Kyle reached down and picked her up. She kept her eyes tightly shut. She didn't want to see him.

'My sweet love, I can't help you if I don't know what's wrong, now can I? There must be something in that tirade you just gave,' he asked reasonably.

'What did you say?' Jenny sat up, eyes wide as she stared into his soft brown ones. 'What did you call me?'

'My sweet love.'

CHAPTER TWELVE

JENNY shook her head. Had she heard right?

'I love you, Jenny Warwick,' said Kyle, looking at her.

'I love you, too,' she answered promptly, a broad smile lighting her face, a singing gladness filling her heart. Kyle loved her!

He drew her up against him again. She rested her cheek against the strong wall of his chest, trailing her fingers down his skin.

'I've loved you for ages, you know,' he murmured softly, lowering his mouth to hers.

'No, I didn't know,' she said, intrigued. 'Since when?'

'Well, let me see.' He cocked his head to one side and gave her his lazy, crooked smile. 'I felt the first stirrings that first winter night. You were so polite to a house-breaker! I found that quite endearing. Then, once I'd been here, everything you did bound me closer to you.'

'Oh, Kyle, I never knew.'

'My darling Jenny, I know that. Your obtuseness has alternated in causing me great amusement and great frustration.'

'But why didn't you tell me?'

He shifted positions a little, resting his chin on her hair, his voice pensive.

'First I wanted this behind us. I wanted to finish the assignment so I could concentrate on just us.

Then, there was some danger, and I wanted you safe from that.'

'And I thought you were after Naomi,' she said.

He chuckled. 'I did wonder once or twice if that was a spark of jealousy I detected, though why I can't say. I paid you a lot of attention. I, on the other hand, didn't know where George fitted in.'

'He's just a friend. I told you.'

'I know that now.'

Jenny lifted her face, eyes shining. 'I think you might have told me before.'

'I wasn't sure how you felt about it. I didn't want to put us in an awkward position before I could be sure of you.'

'You must have suspected once or twice. Surely you don't think I have affairs with men all the time.'

'I was hoping not, but how was I to know? Anyway, it wouldn't have mattered. I want you whatever might have happened in the past. Let me show you.'

His lips closed over hers, warm and exciting. The longing rose in Jenny as his touch, familiar yet exciting, caused her emotions to rise. Slowly he moved against her mouth, tasting the sweetness and delight that was his for the taking. Jenny revelled in his lovemaking, aching to move to more.

She traced his back muscles with her fingertips, then with her nails, drawing them up to the strong column of his neck, feeling the damp curls of his hair. Of course, he'd said he'd just taken a shower. She ran her fingertips lightly down his back to the top of his jeans, back again, delighting in the feel of his warm skin, his hard muscles.

Kyle shivered against her, moving to kiss her cheek, her throat.

'Much more of that, sweetheart, and I won't be responsible for my actions,' he growled in her ear.

Jenny gave him an enchanting smile and said, 'I hope not. What did you have in mind?'

'If you come with me, I'll just show you.'

Kyle led her to his room, his fingers threaded through hers. He paused by the side of the bed and drew her into his strong hold again.

'Do you think I'll ever have enough of you?' he asked against her ear, moving back to her mouth.

She shook her head. 'I sure hope not.' Then she moved to meet his kiss.

Kyle fumbled with the buttons of her shirt, spreading the material, helping her to remove the restraining cloth. She pushed against him with her breasts and knocked him back against the bed, following him down, on top now. Wiggling against him, she deliberately teased him, dropping light kisses, drawing back as he tried to deepen them, rubbing against his chest until he put a stop to it all by rolling over on top of her and pinning her beneath his weight on the mattress.

She giggled up at him, her eyes sparkling with mischief, softening to love as she caught the love in his.

They took their time, playing, loving, teasing. Their passion was not diminished, but heightened by the fun, the pleasure. It was as if they wanted to see how close they could come each time with the teasing before they went over the brink into the ecstasy they knew awaited.

Kyle turned her on her stomach, his hands cupping each firm breast as his mouth slowly kissed, tasted, trailed down each inch of her back, across her shoulders, down her backbone, in the hollows near her waist. Jenny closed her eyes with the sensations he caused, as deep within her the burning began, and spread. The touch of his lips against her satiny skin inciting her, she moved against him, quicker and quicker as the tempo within her built up.

Kyle moved slowly, as if he wanted to touch every bit of her with his mouth, his lips, his tongue.

'I want you,' she whispered, rolling over to face him, reaching up to cup his face in loving hands, to draw him to her. She could not contain the flame within her, wanting him to fan it to the white-hot intensity only Kyle could bring.

'How much do you want me?' he asked, eyes drugged with passion.

'So much I ache,' she answered back, smiling up at him, the loving evident in her eyes.

'Not enough.'

'So much I could die from it.' She reached up to pull him down to her, to rise up and meet him as he thrust against her, revelling in the feel of him, the excitement he engendered.

Jenny was lost again in the conflagration he built in her, floating on the ecstasy he brought; the glorious peaks of each sensuous wave which broke over her again and again.

She was panting when she lay back, the languor beginning to spread through her. She tightened her arms around his neck, fervently kissing him. Not wanting anything to come between them, not even a breath of air.

'I love you, Kyle,' she said simply.

'I love you, Jenny. Marry me soon.'

She smiled sleepily. 'Is that a question, or a command?' she said, rubbing her cheek against his shoulder, trailing her lips against his hot skin.

'Depends,' he growled in her ear, nuzzling her neck. 'If you say yes, it's a question. If there's any doubt, then it's a command.'

'I say yes.'

'When?'

'Just now,' she teased.

'Brat! When will we get married?'

'Whenever you want.' She let her fingers move gently against his back.

'Tomorrow?'

'That soon?'

'Did you have a big wedding with Johnny?'

She nodded.

'Then you don't need one now. No point in waiting, is there?'

'None.' Jenny was silent for a long moment, then she turned her head to see him. 'You don't mind?' she asked.

'What?'

'Me being married before. That you're not the first.'

He took her left hand, gently twisting her ring. 'I'll get you another tomorrow. I want you to wear mine.'

'Yes. I want yours. I do love you, though I did love Johnny. I'm sorry he died. But I can't remember too much of our love now. It's over and gone.

But you make me feel so alive, our love is so alive. I only love you.'

'As long as I'm your last love, I don't mind.'

'And Naomi?' She just had to ask.

He kissed her gently and moved to his side, propped up on his elbow, his legs entwined with hers.

'Still on that? I told you before she was work, only that. I figured she was a lead to who was distributing the pot here in Palmer, or maybe in San Francisco. I told you I never confuse work with pleasure. And you, my darling, were definitely pleasure, the whole way.'

'And where were you last night?' she asked suspiciously.

Kyle laughed, giving her a quick hug. Jenny felt the jolt down to her toes.

'Arresting drug growers left and right. We cracked the case! It's all over now bar the shouting.'

'You didn't tell me! Who was it? What happened?' She watched as his face took on the hard lines he had worn before, then looked pleased.

'It wasn't your friend George Carlisle, if that's what you're worried about.'

'Well, I wasn't worried, exactly, but I'm glad. I've always thought George was nice.'

'But Nate Wilson was one, and Ben Waters. The head guy is some man in Strawberry, Mark Harris. Do you know him?'

Jenny shook her head. 'What happened?'

'We were on the stake-out, and sure enough, just as we'd thought, they came to turn on the water. It was Nate and Ben. We got some good pictures, waited until they were turning off the valve, then arrested them. We've a whole sequence of pictures Ben Waters was scared and spilled the beans. He told us about Mark Harris. We had the Sheriff's office alerted, so when we called for help, they picked up Harris and brought him in.

'I spent the rest of today ploughing up the crop and destroying it. I was up most of last night questioning Waters, then supervised the destruction this morning.'

'When you didn't come back last night, I was worried. I even started to go to the field, but I saw a black car on that road so I decided not to go on.'

'It was probably one of the Sheriff's unmarked cars.'

'I didn't know you were here until I came to make your bed. Your motorcycle isn't in the garage.'

'My bike's still up at the site. We used the Sheriff's car. I'll have to go pick it up later. Naomi gave us some good information about Nate. He's a distributor, as well as grower. Figured to get a bigger percentage, I guess. He had an ideal location for distribution, too. Sooner or later everyone goes to the garage. Anyone stopping there doesn't arouse curiosity.'

'It's hard to believe people I know could be involved in something like this. I'm glad it's over.'

Jenny lay quietly on the bed, closing her eyes, savouring the feel of his hand, warm and heavy on her stomach. His long legs were intertwined with hers, and his breath was soft as it fanned her face.

'Are you going to sleep?' he asked, amused.

'No!' She kept her eyes shut. 'I'm just enjoying lying here with you, having you hold me like this.'

'We can do this a lot when we're married,' he said, dropping a kiss on her forehead.

'Will your family be pleased? I think my mom and dad will be. They like you, though I think they'll be surprised to find you're not Edith's son, after all.'

'My folks will be happy for us. You'll like them, I think, and they'll love you. We'll go down to San Diego in a few days, so everyone can meet.'

'And your sister?' Jenny looked up at him.

Kyle's face closed a little, as if he were looking a long way off, or a long way back. 'She's dead, Jenny. She was a happy sort of person, until the end. She got hooked on hard drugs, through marijuana. I don't think Dad's recovered yet and it's over ten years ago.'

'How awful for you all.'

'That's what got me into this racket. All started from smoking pot. You would have liked her, she was such fun. That's her picture. I always carry it with me, to remind me why I'm doing all this.'

The blonde girl in the picture was his sister! With a feeling of relief and happiness, Jenny reached up to cup his face, pull it down for a soft kiss. 'I love you.'

He smiled down at her. 'You're the best thing that came out of this assignment. I'm glad there was a blizzard last winter.'

'And that you were assigned to it this summer.'

'No, I asked for it especially. Even when I got shot, I made Stuart promise not to give this case to anyone else. I knew when we met last winter that I wanted to see more of you, Jenny. And you,' he laughed softly, 'were a sweetheart. I could have stayed in Strawberry, just as Jason and Mac did. But you were so trusting when we asked for help. I loved it.'

Jenny looked indignant. 'You mean it was all just for your own personal reasons? I wasn't really needed to help with the case?'

'No, I don't mean that at all. We usually don't have the co-operation we got this time. It really helped.'

He smiled again at her self-satisfied look.

'Now what?' she asked, trailing her hand along his back.

'I've got a few days off coming, before my next assignment.'

'What is it?' she asked suspiciously, a small shiver of fear running along her spine.

'I'm switching to the office, no more field work. Too many nights away from home.'

Jenny felt a warm glow spread through her. He would be safe now. She'd be spared the worry and fear for his safety each time he left home. No more anxious waiting to see if he came home safely. She smiled up at him, happiness and love expressed in her look.

'In Sacramento?'

He nodded.

'We could stay here, or move closer,' she suggested. 'It's a wonderful plan. I liked the days-off part, too.'

'Enough to start a honeymoon, always supposing we get married soon.'

'I thought we were.'

'Only if we can get up, and right now I never want to leave the bed.'

He leaned over Jenny, drawing her into his arms and covering her mouth with his.

Jenny returned his kiss, feeling loved, cherished and safe. She would always be so with Kyle.

PAMELA BROWNING

...is fireworks on the green at the Fourth of July and prayers said around the Thanksgiving table. It is the dream of freedom realized in thousands of small towns across this great nation.

But mostly, the Heartland is its people. People who care about and help one another. People who cherish traditional values and give to their children the greatest gift, the gift of love.

American Romance presents HEARTLAND, an emotional trilogy about people whose memories, hopes and dreams are bound up in the acres they farm.

HEARTLAND...the story of America.

Don't miss these heartfelt stories: American Romance #237 SIMPLE GIFTS (March), #241 FLY AWAY (April), and #245 HARVEST HOME (May).

Harlequin Intrigue
Adopts a New Cover Story!

**We are proud to present to you
the new Harlequin Intrigue cover design.**

Look for two exciting new stories each month, which
mix a contemporary, sophisticated romance with the
surprising twists and turns of a puzzler . . . romance
with "something more."

Coming in April
Harlequin Category Romance Specials!

Look for six new and exciting titles from this mix of two genres.

4 Regencies—lighthearted romances set in England's Regency period (1811-1820)

2 Gothics—romance plus suspense, drama and adventure

Regencies

Daughters Four by Dixie Lee McKeone
She set out to matchmake for her sister, but reckoned without the Earl of Beresford's devilish sense of humor.

Contrary Lovers by Clarice Peters
A secret marriage contract bound her to the most interfering man she'd ever met!

Miss Dalrymple's Virtue by Margaret Westhaven
She needed a wealthy patron—and set out to buy one with the only thing she had of value....

The Parson's Pleasure by Patricia Wynn
Fate was cruel, showing her the ideal man, then making it impossible for her to have him....

Gothics

Shadow over Bright Star by Irene M. Pascoe
Did he want her shares to the silver mine, her love—or her life?

Secret at Orient Point by Patricia Werner
They seemed destined for tragedy despite the attraction between them....

CAT88A-1

CAROLE MORTIMER

JUST ONE NIGHT

Hawk Sinclair—Texas millionaire and owner of the exclusive
Sinclair hotels, determined to protect his son's inheritance.
Leonie Spencer—desperate to protect her sister's happiness.

They were together for just one night.
The night their daughter was conceived.

Blackmail, kidnapping and attempted murder add suspense
to passion in this exciting bestseller.

The success story of Carole Mortimer continues with *Just
One Night*, a captivating romance from the author of the
bestselling novels, *Gypsy* and *Merlyn's Magic*.

★

**Available in March
wherever paperbacks are sold.**